LONG SHOTS

THEY BEAT THE ODDS

Jay Jennings

Silver Burdett Press

Published by Silver Burdett Press, Inc., a division of Simon & Schuster, Inc.,
Prentice Hall Bldg., Englewood Cliffs, NJ 07632.

Cover photo: © Andrew Bernstein/NBA
Designer: Greg Wozney
Project Editor: Emily Easton
Manufactured in the United States of America
10 9 8 7 6 5 4 3 2 1

Library of Congress Cataloging-in-Publication Data

Jennings, Jay.
    Long shots / by Jay Jennings.
        p.   cm.
    Includes bibliographical references.
    Contents: Spud Webb — Wilma Rudolph — Shirley Muldowney —
Jim Abbott — The 1969 New York Mets.
    1. Athletes—United States—Biography—Juvenile literature.
2. New York Mets (Baseball team)—History—Juvenile literature.
3. Achievement motivation—Juvenile literature.   [1. Athletes.]
I. Title.
GV697.A1J45   1990
920—dc20
[796′.092′2]
[B]   90-33313
                                                                    CIP
                                                                     AC

ISBN 0-382-24105-3 (LSB)
        0-382-24112-6 (s/c)

Acknowledgments

I could not have written this book without the help of many people. I wish to thank my colleagues at *Sports Illustrated* and other journalists whose work I have drawn from and whose advice I have sought. They include Samuel Abt, Bruce Anderson, Morin Bishop, Robert Creamer, Richard Demak, David Ferroni of DMF Communications, Hank Hersch, Rick Lalor of the National Hot Rod Association, Franz Lidz, Jack McCallum, Roger Mooney, Sam Moses, Rich O'Brien, Jim Reynolds, Steve Rushin, Ed Swift, Julie Vader, Alex Wolff and Jane Wulf.

Special thanks go out to my editor, Emily Easton; Ken Young, who steered the project my way; my agent Kris Dahl at International Creative Management; and her assistant Gordon Kato.

Most of all, I wish to thank my wife Jessica Green for her constant encouragement, her attentive reading of the manuscript and her belief in me. *Senza lei, niente.*

Photo Acknowledgments

Allsport USA: Pages vi (Allsport USA/Damian Strohmeyer) 17, 20 (Allsport USA/Konig), 22 (Allsport USA/Mike Scully), 27 (Allsport USA/Ralph Merlino), 29 (Allsport USA/Mike Scully), 32 (Allsport USA/Robert Beck), 34 (Allsport USA/Kirk Schlea), 38 (Allsport USA/Joe Patronite).

Louis DeLuca: Pages 5, 7.

Focus on Sports: Pages 30, 41 (Focus on Sports/Michael Ponzini), 44, 49, 50, 52

Jessica Green: Page iv.

NBA/Andrew Bernstein: Page 8.

Sports Illustrated: Page 10 (Marvin E. Newman/Sports Illustrated).

Wide World Photos, Inc.: Page 18.

FROM THE AUTHOR

Sports writers and fans use the term "long shot" to identify someone who they think has only a slight chance of winning. Because successful athletes generally have tremendous self-confidence, I don't believe those profiled here would use that term about themselves. Still, *Long Shots* is an appropriate title for this book because these athletes overcam greater obstacles than most in rising to excel in their sports.

To athletes, surmounting a great barrier to succeed is simply a part of doing what they love. In addition to mastering the complexities of their individual sports, the athletes included here faced more difficult challenges, such as injury, physical limitations, racism, and sexism. Most of all, they heard people tell them over and over that the odds were too great, they they should give up. They didn't listen to the skeptics. That is what makes them winners and what makes their lives worth reading about.

We, the sports fans who watch these athletes perform on television or who read about their triumphs, only know the end result. We watch basketball player Spud Webb fly through the air for a dunk. We read how drag racer Shirley Muldowney roared down a quarter-mile racetrack in record time. We see baseball pitcher Jim Abbott field a bunt cleanly and throw out the runner even though he was born without a right hand. To us these feats are amazing. To the athletes they are merely the sum of determination, experience, and hard work.

The athletes chosen for this book have been drawn from a variety of sports. It is my hope that readers who pick up the book for an inspiring baseball story will also be moved and impressed by the stories of the athletes in less familiar sports, like drag racing.

I also hope that readers who have been told that they are long shots (in sports or any other endeavor) will look to the examples here and be inspired to prove the doubters wrong.

Jay Jennings

CONTENTS

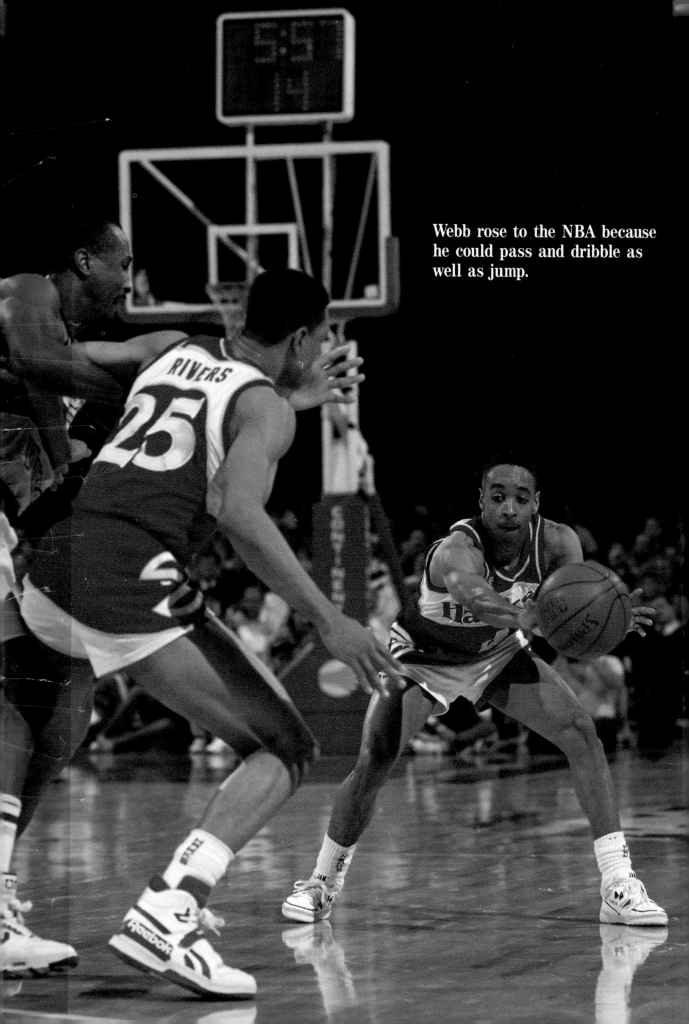

Webb rose to the NBA because he could pass and dribble as well as jump.

SPUD WEBB

Basketball's Little Big Man

David and Katie Webb own Webb's Soul Market, a store near the Cotton Bowl football stadium in Dallas, Texas. On February 8, 1986, for the first time in a long while, they hired someone other than a family member to work the cash register. They took the short drive to Reunion Arena, which was the site of the National Basketball Association's All-Star Game. Their son, Anthony "Spud" Webb, at the time the smallest player in NBA history, was going to compete in the league's slam-dunk contest.

Only a few months before, no one could have imagined that Webb would be on the same floor with the best dunkers in the league, many of whom were more than a foot taller than he. In fact, few people believed he could even play in the NBA. But here he was in his hometown, ready to try to dunk against the league's most exciting, aerodynamic players—including his own friend and teammate on the Atlanta Hawks, Dominique Wilkins.

All his life Webb had been told he was too small to play basketball, and he had steadfastly refused to believe it. Now he had the chance to prove to everyone who had doubted him that he belonged with the best. But it wasn't enough for him to just be there. He wanted to win.

When Anthony Jerome Webb was born in 1963, the fifth of six children, he had very little hair, and a friend of the family thought that his head looked like a sputnik, the spacecraft that the Russians had launched in the late 1950s and early 1960s. The family affectionately called him "Sputnikhead" and this later was shortened to "Spud." He has been known by that name ever since.

He was always smaller than other kids his age. In his autobiography, *Flying High*, he wrote, "Being the smallest was something I slowly began to accept, yet it frustrated me. I always thought, if I were just a little bit bigger, I could be a much better athlete."

Growing up, Webb played football, took up boxing, and even shot pool in his parents' store. By the time he was twelve, basketball was becoming his favorite sport, even though he was only 4'9" and weighed just 90 pounds. He played often at the local Boys Club. He used his quickness against taller opponents, darting past them for **lay-ups** or sneaking in for a steal.

Starting for his junior high team, he began to see his size as an advantage. He wrote, again in *Flying High*, "In some ways, I think being small was an asset early on, because I was comfortable with my body, while the bigger, ganglier kids were still growing like weeds and as a result were very uncoordinated."

When he got to Wilmer-Hutchins High School, the coaches frowned at his size. He was assigned to the junior varsity for his first two years and played well. But when the time came to pick the varsity during his junior year, Webb wasn't on the list. He was so disappointed he almost quit. He didn't want to play another year on the junior varsity (j.v.) team, but he decided to stick with it and try his best to make the varsity for his senior year.

Between his junior and senior years, Webb began training furiously. He ran all around his South Dallas neighborhood and played basketball in the local gyms for hours. After their games, all the players would line up for dunking practice. Webb tried day after day, but he was only 5'3". His legs, however, were getting stronger from the constant running and jumping.

Finally, all his training paid off. One day, after weeks of getting close, he flew toward the rim and stuffed the ball. All his friends congratulated him.

When tryouts for varsity basketball were held in the fall, Webb surprised the coach by stealing the ball from an opponent, streaking downcourt, and throwing down a dunk. The coach couldn't ignore him now.

Webb made the varsity and started the entire year, leading his team to a 27–9 record. He had averaged 26 points per game and had been selected to the All-Metro and All-State teams. He even played in the Texas High School All-Star Game.

Despite his high scoring average and his dunking ability, only one four-year college, North Texas State University, offered Webb a scholarship. He thought he had enough talent to play with a better team. No one else did. He was hurt that coaches at other schools didn't believe in him.

As a result, he chose to attend a junior college first and then transfer when he had proved himself there and improved his play. Many athletes attend two-year colleges to help them develop their athletic skills and to get used to college-level schoolwork. Webb thought if he could play well in a junior college, he could get a scholarship to a university that played in one of the best conferences.

He decided to attend Midland College, a junior college 325 miles west of Dallas. He knew he could make the starting team right away.

That first season, he did play a lot. As his team's **point guard**, the man who directs the offense, Webb averaged 20.8 points and 7.1 assists a game. His great leaping ability allowed him to block 20 shots. He was even called for 2 **goaltending** violations when he swatted away shots on their downward path to the basket. Usually only the tallest players, 6'10" centers and 6'7" forwards, have the ability to do that.

The most impressive number of all during his first year was his tally of over 40 dunks. But Webb didn't care much for individual statistics. He wanted the team to do well.

The team, coached by Jerry Stone, played well enough during the year to make it to the National Junior College Athletic Association tournament in Hutchinson, Kansas. Every year the sixteen best teams meet there for a play-off to determine a national champion.

The Midland fans already knew about Webb's extraordinary talents. At the tournament, many of them wore buttons which read, I'M A SPUD NUT. The other fans in Hutchinson soon found out about him. During a first-round game, Webb stole a pass and sped downcourt for a powerful, one-handed, rim-shaking dunk. The crowd went crazy at seeing such an exciting play. Coach Stone told *Sports Illustrated* magazine, "Before that, Spud was a rumor; after it, he was real."

Midland made it all the way to the final game against Miami–Dade North Community College from Florida. Miami was undefeated and ranked as the No. 1 junior college team in the country. Hutchinson Arena was packed with boisterous fans.

At halftime Midland was leading by 4 points. Just as no one expected Webb to be a good basketball player, no one expected Midland to be able to keep up with Miami. But Midland was winning.

In the second half coach Stone put in a strategy that gave Webb even greater control over the team. Miami had more talented players than Midland, so their starters were able to rest without losing ground to Midland. On the other hand, Midland had used nearly the same five

players for the whole first half. To give his players some time to rest, Stone put in an offense the Boston Celtics of the NBA used in the 1950s when they had brilliant ball-handling guard Bob Cousy. Even when guarded closely by the defense, Cousy had the ability to dribble away from the opposition or make a quick pass to an open man. As long as he had the ball in his hands, it was unlikely that the other team could steal it from him.

The center would come out to the free throw line and pass the ball to Webb, who would dribble around until he saw an opening in the defense. Then he would fire a pass inside or drive through an opening to the basket. This offense worked perfectly against Miami's **zone defense**, in which Miami players covered a particular area, or "zone", of the court rather than an opposing player.

Desperately trying to get the ball away from Webb, Miami players committed fouls against him, and he hit 18 out of 20 free throws. Regulation play ended with the score tied, so the two teams went into overtime.

With only 14 seconds left in the extra period, Miami was leading by 2 and Midland had the ball. Webb drove to the basket and took a jump shot from 10 feet as Midland's 6'10" center jumped out at him. The ball sailed over the center's outstretched arms and fell through the hoop to tie the game. A second overtime period would be required.

Webb keyed the Midland offense in the second overtime. He dashed past two Miami players and arched his shot over a third to give his team an 86-81 lead. The crowd erupted. Miami came back down the court and scored, but Webb answered by picking up a loose ball and flying in for the lay-up. That gave Midland a five-point lead.

In a desperate attempt to cut into that lead, Miami fouled Midland players, but Webb's teammates hit the free throws. As the final seconds ticked off, the scoreboard read 93-88 in favor of Midland. Webb

HOOP TALK

assist: a pass that results in a score. The player passing the ball is credited with an assist.

goaltending: a rule-breaking move in which a player interferes with a shot as it travels on a downward path to the basket. The shooter is awarded two points.

lay-up: a running one-handed shot close to the basket in which the player either drops the ball over the rim or uses the backboard to bank the ball into the basket.

point guard: the player who directs the team when it is trying to score points, setting up plays and passing the ball to other players.

zone defense: a strategy for guarding an opposing team in which players are assigned areas of the court to cover rather than individual opposing players. This type of defense is not legal in professional basketball.

finished with 36 points.

Midland received the championship trophy and a standing ovation from the crowd. But there was one more trophy to be awarded: the Bud Obee Outstanding Small Player Award, given to the best small player in the tournament. Tournament director Al Wagler joked, "This is probably the most difficult decision we've had to make." Everyone in the crowd laughed. They all knew the prize could go to only one player, Spud Webb.

The underdogs had done it, and the littlest underdog had proved that he was not just a leaping wonder but a complete player. That's how he likes to be known. He told *Sports Illustrated*, "People talk about my dunking and not the other stuff. I can pass, jump-shoot, dribble, lead the team. Maybe they want entertainment, but I want to be known as a good point guard."

Still, there were doubters. He's a good player at the junior college level, people said, but could he compete at a major university where the competition is stiffer? Webb had high hopes and confidence in himself, but even after his great freshman year, no major college offered him a scholarship. He returned to Midland.

Though Webb was a Junior College All-America as a sophomore, the team didn't have the spark of the year before and didn't do as well. And only a few small four-year schools were interested in Webb's talents.

Then, almost out of the blue, Webb got a call from an assistant coach at North Carolina State University named Tom Abatemarco. The N.C. State Wolfpack plays in the Atlantic Coast Conference, one of the best conferences in the country. They had won the national championship of their division the year before, but their point guard had finished his career, and a recruit the coaches had been counting on had decided to attend another school. Abatemarco had read about Webb in a magazine and decided to invite him to visit the school.

There's a funny story about Webb's arrival in North Carolina. Abatemarco and head coach Jim Valvano were to meet Webb at Raleigh-Durham Airport. When Valvano saw Webb approaching them in the terminal and noticed how small he was, Valvano turned to Abatemarco and said, "Tom, if that kid is Spud Webb, then you're fired." Valvano was joking, and the two men laughed, but the story shows that Webb constantly has to overcome the assumption that a small man is not physically suited for playing basketball.

Webb's first game for N.C. State was the Hall of Fame Tipoff Classic, played in Springfield, Massachusetts. Dr. James Naismith invented the game of basketball there in 1891, and every year the city hosts a game between two of the finest college teams in the country.

There was a lot of pressure on Webb. For the first time, he would be playing on national television. He didn't let that bother him. N.C. State won the game 76–64 against the University of Houston, and Webb scored 18 points, dished out 5 **assists**, pulled down 4 rebounds and had 3 steals. He was also named the game's most valuable player. On one spectacular play, he sped the length of the court and put in a lay-up over Akeem Olajuwon, Houston's 7-foot center.

The nation was learning about Spud Webb. During that year, he received bundles of mail. Webb wrote in his autobiography, "Mail call was among my favorite times of the day. Much of it was from young fans, small kids who like me had been told to take up a sport other than basketball. Those letters always lifted my spirits."

N.C State had a mediocre season, but Webb averaged 9.8 points per game and led the conference with 199 assists. More important, he showed everyone that he could play with the best college players in the nation.

During his senior year, the team enjoyed greater success and Webb continued to surprise those skeptics who still said he was oo short. During one game against Clemson University, he even had 8 rebounds.

Perhaps his sweetest revenge came during N.C. State's game against Southern Methodist University, which is located in Webb's hometown of Dallas. Though he played high school basketball in the same city, SMU hadn't bothered to recruit him. He showed them what they had missed by scoring 17 points and handing out 10 assists as the Wolfpack won.

That season also provided another interesting challenge for Webb in N.C.

State's games against Wake Forest University. He had to compete against a smaller player, 5'3" Tyrone "Muggsy" Bogues, who is also now playing in the NBA for the Charlotte Hornets. In one game, Webb scored 18 points and Bogues scored 20, proving that there is a place for the little man in what's frequently called a big man's game.

N.C. State finished the season with a 23–10 record. Webb had a superb senior year, averaging 11.1 points and 5.3 assists per game. Under his leadership, the team

At the 1986 dunk contest, Webb's slams amazed both fans and players.

won three games in the national collegiate tournament.

The next step for Webb was perhaps the most unlikely of all. No one as small as he had ever played in the NBA. In the late 1940s Wat Misaka and Red Klotz both measured in at 5'7" but weighed 150 pounds and only played in a handful of games each. Calvin Murphy of the Houston Rockets is remembered as perhaps the best little man to play in recent years, but he was 5'9" and a stocky 165 pounds. Critics who were impressed with Webb's speed and jumping ability thought he was too slight to endure the NBA's physical style of play. Because NBA rules do not allow zone defenses, players guard each other more closely. Therefore body contact and collisions occur more frequently. A player has to be strong to match up with the other players. Webb is 5' 5½" (5' 7" in his socks and sneakers) and weighs only 133 pounds.

During the NBA's draft of college players in 1985, the Detroit Pistons decided to take a chance on him, even though they had one of the best small guards in the history of the league in 6-foot-tall Isiah Thomas. The Pistons then changed their minds about Webb and released him from their roster before training camp even opened.

But another small man in the league had his eye on Webb. Mike Fratello, the Atlanta Hawks' coach, who stands only 5'7", invited Webb to come to the Hawks' training camp. The Hawks had a shortage of guards, and Webb would provide depth. He performed well in preseason and made the team. The kid who hadn't made his high school varsity team until his senior year was now on an NBA roster.

The first dunk of his NBA career came on opening night in Atlanta before 10,129 fans. In the third quarter, he stole a pass and darted downcourt, blowing past the guards of the Washington Bullets. They looked on from midcourt as he rose to the full height of his jump and threw the ball through the basket.

He would have many highlights during his first season as Atlanta's backup point guard. In February, with one of the Hawks' starting guards out with an injury, Webb started against the NBA champion Los Angeles Lakers. Against that team famous for its running style of play, Webb zipped over, around, and through them for 23 points and 13 assists. Laker coach Pat Riley said after the game, "He's one of the great athletes of our time. He's got great quickness, great jumping ability, and he's fearless."

The next game he had 22 points and 15 assists against Cleveland.

The fans in Atlanta loved him. The management of the team decided to honor him with Spud Webb Sticker Night— because, as one team official said, he's too small for a poster.

The crowning moment of his rookie year came during the league's All-Star weekend, which by coincidence was being held in his hometown, Dallas. Word had got out about his jumping ability, and Webb was invited to compete in the slam-dunk contest held the day before the All-Star Game. No one, except for Webb himself, expected him to win. When he was introduced to the crowd, other players were laughing and patting him playfully on the head.

The contest is scored by judges who rate the players on style and flair, the way diving and figure skating judges rate competitors in those sports. Julius Erving, also known as Dr. J, was the greatest dunker of all, combining the strength and grace of a ballet dancer in his moves. His stylishness made the dunk the most popular and thrilling shot in basketball. Dr. J was the biggest star in the old American Basketball Association, from which the NBA borrowed the idea of a dunk contest.

In his first attempt, Webb, who was 10 inches shorter than any other contestant, ran toward the right side of the basket, leapt and turned around in the air with his back to the net. He then dunked the ball so hard behind his head that after the ball went through the net, it hit the top of his head and bounced back out of the rim. Everyone knew that Webb was there to win.

By the end of the competition, the only two dunkers left were Webb and his teammate Dominique Wilkins, who had won the contest the year before and has been called "The Human Highlight Film." Wilkins' powerful slams usually leave the backboard shaking.

Being a teammate, Wilkins knew what Webb could do. The little man had already performed two dunks during which he spun around in the air in a full circle before dunking. That is called a "360" because the player rotates 360 degrees before slamming the ball through the hoop.

As Webb stood holding the ball at halfcourt, he was thinking about his final dunk. The crowd was buzzing. Was there anything he could do that they hadn't already seen?

Still standing near the halfcourt line, he lofted the ball high into the air so that it would land near the free throw line and bounce up toward the goal. He then ran toward the basket himself, following the arc of the ball with intense eyes. When the ball bounced close to the basket, he leapt, made a half-turn in the air, and caught the ball in front of his face. With his back now facing the hoop, he kicked out his right leg to give himself one more boost and drove the ball hard through the center of the rim behind his head.

The crowd exploded. The other players were laughing and giving each other high-fives. The five judges each gave him a score of 10, a total of 50 points for the dunk, the best score possible. Wilkins had one dunk left, and though it was a good one, he got a total of only 48. Webb had won.

Spud Webb is, however, more than a champion dunker. As improbable as winning that contest might seem, it is even more unlikely that Webb has remained in the NBA as a regular player, doing more than dunking. He can leap, yes, but he also possesses skills that make him a complete basketball player. And if he hadn't developed those skills enough to make a team, he would never have been able to compete in the dunk contest.

The odds, and the law of gravity, were against Spud Webb. He has defied them both.

As a point guard, Webb is always looking for the open man.

Though he is only 5′5½″, Webb stands tall for the Atlanta Hawks.

FOR THE EXTRA POINT

Aaseng, Nathan. *Little Giants of Pro Sports*.
Minneapolis, Minnesota: Lerner Books, 1980.

Webb, Spud, with Reid Slaughter. *Flying High*.
New York: Harper & Row, 1988. (Advanced
Readers.)

Zodra, Dan. *The Atlanta Hawks*. Mankato,
Minnesota: Creative Education, 1988.

ANTHONY JEROME "SPUD" WEBB

COLLEGE STATISTICS

Midland Junior College
Chaparrals

Season	Games	Points	Average	Assists	Average
1981–82	38	789	20.8	271	7.1
1982–83	35	512	14.6	355	10.1
Totals	73	1301	17.8	626	8.6

North Carolina State University
Wolfpack

Season	Games	Points	Average	Assists	Average
1983–84	33	323	9.8	199	6.0
1984–85	33	366	11.1	174	5.3
Totals	66	689	10.4	373	5.6

NATIONAL BASKETBALL ASSOCIATION STATISTICS

Atlanta Hawks
Regular Season

Season	Games	Points	Average	Assists	Average
1985–86	79	616	7.8	337	4.3
1986–87	33	223	6.8	167	5.1
1987–88	82	490	6.0	337	4.1
1988–89	81	319	3.9	284	3.5
Totals	275	1648	6.0	1125	4.1

Play-offs

Season	Games	Points	Average	Assists	Average
1985–86	9	110	12.2	65	7.2
1986–87	8	31	3.9	38	4.8
1987–88	12	106	8.8	56	4.7
1988–89	5	8	1.6	15	3.0
Totals	34	255	7.5	174	5.1

Rudolph impressed crowds not only with her speed but with her grace.

WILMA RUDOLPH

Track's
Golden Gazelle

The picture of Wilma Rudolph crossing the finish line during the 1960 Olympics would become familiar to the world. Television, newspapers, and magazines caught her in her characteristic pose. With her chin raised in the air, she extended her torso, which was covered with the letters "U. S. A." Her arms were bent but relaxed; her 6-foot frame leaned dramatically forward. But dominating the picture were her long, powerful legs, which propelled her faster than any woman had ever run.

Less than a decade before, one of those legs had been in a metal brace, and the girl who would become the world's fastest woman could barely walk.

Wilma Glodean Rudolph was born on June 23, 1940, in St. Bethlehem, Tennessee, a rural farming community about 50 miles from Nashville. Her father, Ed, was a railroad porter and her mother, Blanche, worked as a domestic maid. Shortly after Wilma was born, the family moved into a cottage in Clarksville, Tennessee, a town about four miles away with a population of sixteen thousand people. The Rudolphs were a large and loving family; Wilma was the sixth of eight children born to Blanche and Ed. Wilma's father also had eleven children from a previous marriage.

From the beginning, Wilma overcame tremendous odds. She was born two months early and weighed only 4½ pounds. Such babies often get sick more easily, even with the best medical care, and Wilma suffered from one dangerous illness after another.

Growing up poor and black in the South of the 1940s, before blacks had gained many of the rights they hold today, made the situation worse. There was only one black doctor in all of Clarksville then. By the time Wilma was three, she had already suffered from mumps, measles, and chicken pox. With advances in medicine, these childhood diseases have become easily treatable with vaccines and medications that were not available when Wilma was a baby.

Her worst bout with illness came during the next year, when she was four. Wilma had double pneumonia followed by scarlet fever, and she nearly died. When she finally recovered from those sicknesses, her left leg was slightly deformed.

Wilma's doctors didn't think that she would ever regain the use of her leg, but that didn't keep Wilma and her mother from hoping and from doing something about it. Twice a week, six-year-old Wilma and her mother boarded a Greyhound bus and rode 45 miles into Nashville to the Meharry Medical College, the nearest black hospital. Because Wilma and her mother were black, they were not allowed to ride in the front of the bus. This separation of blacks and whites extended to schools, restaurants, hospitals, and even drinking fountains. Doctors at Meharry massaged the leg and put Wilma through a program of physical therapy to strengthen the muscles.

When her mother asked the doctors what more she could do to help, they taught her the massaging technique so she could treat Wilma at home. Her mother in turn taught Wilma's brothers and sisters the technique, and everyone took turns working on Wilma's leg.

In addition to the treatment, Wilma had to wear a heavy metal brace to help straighten the leg. While her brothers and sisters were playing, Wilma could only watch them from a chair. At home, she hopped around the house, dragging her brace with her, trying to remain cheerful.

At age seven, she was able to move well enough to attend Cobb Elementary School. She was happy to be out of the house, but she had to learn to deal with the teasing from kids who made fun of her leg. She tried not to let anything discourage her. She practiced walking normally to make her leg less apparent. While the other children played their games, Wilma watched them, playing the game in her mind, thinking about their mistakes and plotting how she could have done better.

Gradually, by the time she was ten, she was able to remove the brace for a few hours a day. She wore it less and less through the next two years, as her leg began to grow normally. Then one day her mother wrapped up the brace and sent it back to the hospital. Wilma would never have to wear it again. The hours of massage, work-outs at the hospital, and most of all Wilma's determination had completely healed her leg. Six long years in the brace; now she was finally free.

So, with more than the usual enthusiasm, thirteen-year-old Wilma bounded up the steps of her new school. She was entering the seventh grade at Burt High School, which blacks in Clarksville attended until the twelfth grade. For the first time her legs were free.

After waiting and watching for so long, she jumped into sports, especially basketball, with unlimited energy and excitement. Wilma's older sister Yvonne had played basketball for coach Clinton Gray at Burt High, and Wilma wanted to follow in her footsteps. Because she was new to the game that other kids had been playing for years, Wilma's skills developed slowly. She was, however, tall and coordinated despite her years in the brace.

Though it was soon obvious that she was a talented athlete, Gray didn't let her play in games very often. Wilma studied the action from the bench, worked hard in practices, and continued to add to her knowledge of the game. She had learned from her therapy that sometimes rewards come only after years of patience and hard work.

By the time she was a sophomore, Wilma had earned a starting spot on the basketball team. That year she averaged 32.1 points per game and led Burt High to the state high school championship tournament in Nashville. Though her team lost in the second round, something happened there that would change her life.

One of the referees in the game was Ed Temple, the track coach at Tennessee State University, a black college in Nashville. He was an ambitious young man who had built the Tennessee State Tigerbelles into one of the best women's track teams in the country. Refereeing high school basketball games allowed him to look at the best athletes in the state and find young women who might be potential track stars. Each summer he worked with several high school–aged athletes to help them develop their skills. If they were good enough, when they finished twelfth grade he would offer them a scholarship to the college.

He noticed the grace and speed that Wilma showed on the court and thought that she could be an even better **sprinter** than basketball player. Her long legs were perfect for covering the short distances (100 and 200 meters) that a sprinter runs.

She had already run track for a couple of years at Burt High, but the meets were generally informal and the races untimed. She had no idea how fast she was running when she won.

Later that year, in 1956, she attended a track meet sponsored by the Amateur Athletic Union (AAU) and held at the Tuskegee Institute in Alabama. The college was founded by the black educator Booker T. Washington in 1881 and was one of the first institutions of higher learning for blacks in the United States.

Wilma's lack of formal coaching in track hurt her performance. She didn't win a single race. After seeing the better-trained runners she was competing against, she

TRACK TALK

anchor: the final runner of a relay race; sometimes called the anchor leg or anchor position.

qualifying heat: an early round of competition in which the winners move on to the next level and the losers are eliminated.

relay: a race between two or more teams, in which each member of the team runs a part of the race, passing a baton to the next member until the total distance is completed.

sprinter: a runner who competes over short distances, such as the 100 and 200 meters. Because they don't have to pace themselves to cover a longer distance, sprinters usually run faster than long-distance runners.

starting blocks: two foot supports that a sprinter pushes off of at the start of a race.

now realized that her raw talent would only take her so far. She needed proper training to help her succeed.

Despite her poor performance in Alabama, Temple came through with an offer. He approached Wilma and asked her to train during the summer on the Tennessee State campus in Nashville. She discussed it with her parents, and they agreed that it was an opportunity she shouldn't pass up. Not only would she learn more about track and improve her athletic skills, she would also have the chance to earn a scholarship to college, which her parents would never have been able to afford.

By listening to Temple and watching some of the more experienced college runners, she learned during that summer how to run with her muscles relaxed, how to avoid all wasted motion, and how to use the starting blocks. Conditioning drills, such as sprinting up and down the stadium stairs and cross-country running, built up her stamina.

By the end of the summer, Temple decided to include Wilma on a team of junior Tigerbelles traveling to compete in the National AAU meet in Philadelphia, Pennsylvania. She won the 75- and 100-yard dashes. In the 440-yard **relay**, Temple placed her in the **anchor position**, or the final leg of the race, which is usually reserved for the fastest runner. Her team won that race as well.

After the meet, she and her teammates were introduced to Jackie Robinson, the first black to play major league baseball. He told her, "You are a fascinating runner and don't let anybody or anything keep you from running. Keep running."

Wilma continued to improve, so much so that Temple asked her to come to Seattle, Washington, and run in the upcoming U.S. trials for the 1956 Olympic Games. She didn't really know what the Olympics were and had never heard of Melbourne, Australia, the site of the Games that year, but she agreed to go.

Temple and the Tigerbelles made the long drive from Nashville to Seattle. Wilma had never been that far away from home before, and one of the older Tigerbelles, Mae Faggs, took the nervous sixteen-year-old under her wing. Faggs, herself a veteran of two Olympics, encouraged Rudolph and the two became friends.

Just before the **qualifying heat** for the 200 meters, the race that would determine the runners for the Olympic team, as Rudolph related in her autobiography, *Wilma*, Faggs told her, "Concentrate on doing nothing else but sticking with me." The two runners hit the finish line at exactly the same time, finishing in a tie. Both qualified for the team. Just a few months before, Rudolph hadn't been able to beat runners her own age in a regional meet. And just four years before that, she was still wearing a brace on her leg. Now she had earned a place among the best sprinters in the country and would compete against the best in the world.

Because Australia is in the Southern Hemisphere, the summer occurs during what are winter months in the Northern Hemisphere. So in November, Wilma and the U. S. Olympic team flew to Melbourne for the Summer Olympics. In the Olympic quarters for the athletes, Rudolph was fascinated by the people she met from all over the world. Athletes from different countries compared their cultures and learned to communicate, even without the common bond of language.

She was entered in the 200 meters and the 4×100-meter relay. Runners have to finish well in several early races, called qualifying heats, in order to advance to the final race for the gold medal. Disappointed when she only advanced to the semi-final, heat in the 200 meters, the last heat before the finals, Rudolph wanted to prove herself in the relay. She ran the third leg, and the U.S. team, which had been expected to finish no better than fifth, won a bronze medal by coming in third behind the Australian and British teams.

She was happy to get a medal, but the one bronze medal did not satisfy her. She vowed to herself to compete in the next Olympics, in Rome four years later, and promised herself she would do better.

The long trip back to the U.S. and on to Clarksville was tiring. The town held a special reception for her, but she didn't want any special treatment. She just loved to compete. Wilma even asked Coach Gray if she could play in Burt High's basketball game that night. At heart, the young woman who had won a bronze medal still loved high school sports.

Wilma's success in athletics did not protect her from tragedy. On the night of the Burt High School prom at the end of the school year, her best friend, who was a basketball teammate, was killed in an automobile accident. The loss devastated Wilma. She returned the following summer to work out with Coach Temple in Nashville, but thoughts of her friend remained a constant distraction. She poured herself into her training and was able in time to accept the fact of her friend's death. She wrote in her autobiography, "Slowly, I started coming out of it; being in another city, in another atmosphere, helped me do it."

Wilma returned to Clarksville for her senior year at Burt High. Like every high school senior, she looked forward to having her best year both on and off the track and basketball court. She had everything a young girl growing up in the 1950s could want. She was intelligent, athletic, and had a steady boyfriend, a classmate named Robert Eldridge, whom she would eventually marry in 1963.

The year took a different turn when she went to the doctor for a routine physical checkup before basketball season. After the examination, the doctor told her to come back in a couple of days for a private conference. During her next visit to the doctor, he gave her some startling news: She was pregnant. Wilma was shocked. She recalled in her autobiography, "Pregnant? I couldn't understand it. Robert and I had just started to get involved in sex, and here I was pregnant. We were both innocent about sex, didn't know anything about birth control or about contraceptives."

During the time Wilma was in high school, society was much less open about sex, especially in small towns like Clarksville. Churches played a major role in such towns, and many of them objected to any kind of frank discussions about sex. Sex education was rarely taught in the schools. The only way to learn about sex was from parents, and the parents were often afraid or unsure about how to talk to their children about it.

Wilma decided to confide in her sister Yvonne, who broke the news to their mother. Mrs. Rudolph then told their father. The reactions she got from her parents surprised and pleased her. Her mother, she wrote, "said she'd stick with me, no matter

what. My father said two things, 'One, no more Robert; I forbid you to see him again. Two, don't worry about anything, don't be ashamed of anything, everybody makes mistakes.'" Though she loved Robert and was upset that her father wouldn't let her see him, she had thought he would react more harshly.

Temple also stood by his star runner. He had a rule that no athlete who had had a baby could run on his track team, but he agreed to suspend the rule so that Wilma could still attend Tennessee State on scholarship and be a Tigerbelle.

At the Burt High graduation ceremony in May of 1958, Wilma was seven months pregnant. But thanks to the love and support of her family and friends, she held her head high as she accepted her diploma. And she looked forward to the challenges ahead of her—becoming a mother and training for the 1960 Olympics.

Yolanda, the daughter of Wilma and Robert, was born in July of 1958. Wilma's mother and sister agreed to care for Yolanda while Wilma was in Nashville at school. Even though Temple allowed her on the team, he didn't give her any special treatment because she was a mother. Often she wanted to take time off to see her baby in Clarksville, and Temple refused to let her because none of the other girls were allowed to leave campus.

Her freshman year was not an easy one. She was studying elementary education and psychology and had to keep up her grades in order to keep her scholarship. Track and studies took up most of her time. In addition, she missed Yolanda terribly. At times she wanted to just give up track, move back to Clarksville and start a family. But, as she later wrote, "I really didn't want to become a housewife at such an early age, I knew I could still be a runner, and I wanted to be able to go to the Olympics in 1960." She kept her eyes focused on the goal of a gold medal.

In the year before the Olympics, Wilma

let nothing interfere with her goal. Yolanda was settled with the Rudolphs in Clarksville, Wilma's studies were under control, and she was running faster than ever.

In May 1960, at the national AAU indoor meet in Chicago, Illinois, she set American records in the 100- and 220-yard dashes, running the former in 10.7 seconds and the latter in 25.7 seconds. In late June, she set new American outdoor records at an AAU meet in Cleveland, Ohio, running the 100-yard dash in 10.6 seconds and the 220-yard dash in 23.9.

The next month the National AAU meet was held in Corpus Christi, Texas. It was the last major meet in preparation for the 1960 Olympic trials, which would be held in late July in Abilene, Texas. In the blazing heat of a South Texas summer, Rudolph glided through the 200 meters with her gazellelike strides and finished in 22.9 seconds for a new world record.

At the Olympic trials, Rudolph won the 100- and 200-meter dashes. Five of her Tigerbelle teammates won places on the team. To the joy of Rudolph and the other Tennessee State athletes, Ed Temple was named coach of the Olympic team. As unlikely as it seemed, the demanding coach and a group of his athletes from a small black college in Tennessee would be traveling to Rome.

For Rudolph, there was a world of difference between the Melbourne Olympics in 1956 and the Rome Olympics in 1960. She would be on the other side of the globe from Australia in one of civilization's oldest cities. And her own world had undergone change as well. She was a woman, a mother, and a college student instead of a young high school girl. In Rome, with four more years of maturity and experience as a sprinter, she was ready to bring home gold medals instead of a bronze.

The weather in Rome was hot, and it reminded Rudolph and her teammates of their summers training in Tennessee.

Having Temple there also made Rudolph and the other Tigerbelles feel at home. He knew when they were worried and upset, when to be stern with them, and when to soothe them. Every sign seemed favorable for the American women's team to give its best showing since it won six track and field events in the 1932 Games.

Relaxed and comfortable on the day before she was supposed to run in her first race—an early heat of the 100 meters—Rudolph and some teammates were jogging on a grassy field behind Olympic Stadium. The sprinklers were on, and with the temperature in the 100s, the woman decided to playfully run through them to cool off. Jumping over one sprinkler, Rudolph landed in a hole she hadn't noticed. Her left ankle turned and she fell in a heap on the ground. The others rushed over to help and saw that the ankle was swollen and discolored. All Rudolph saw was her dreams of gold fading. Back in her room the trainer tended to her, taping and raising the ankle to prevent swelling. The injury was only a sprain, not a break. The next morning she was able to put weight on it without feeling much pain. She was relieved that it didn't hurt and was confident she could perform well.

The Olympic Stadium was packed with eighty thousand fans when Rudolph entered. She looked serene on the outside, showing no emotion, but she was very nervous. She tested the heavily taped ankle with one practice start; it still didn't hurt. Matched against lesser competition, she won the heat easily. In a later heat that day, she won again. Now she could rest her ankle until the two heats the following day.

She won her first heat that day, the last preliminary before the final, and she was feeling loose and confident. She covered the distance in 11.3 seconds, equalling the world record.

In the 100-meter final, Rudolph's main challenger would be Dorothy Hyman of Great Britain. Once again the stadium was filled on the day of the finals. The international media had become enchanted with Rudolph. The Italian press called her "La Gazzella Nera," or the Black Gazelle. French journalists dubbed her "La Chattanooga Choo Choo," linking her Tennessee upbringing and locomotive speed to a popular American song. Many in the crowd simply chanted her name: "Wil-ma! Wil-ma!"

Before the start, many of the runners nervously shook their hands and kicked their legs. Rudolph stood still, conserving her energy and looking the other runners in the eye. The contestants took their places in the **starting blocks** as the crowd hushed.

The gun sounded and Rudolph got off to a good start, about the third one out of the starting blocks. Gradually she passed those ahead of her, picking up speed as she always did in the last 50 meters. She finished a full

Rudolph's heavily-taped left ankle didn't hurt her in the 200 meters.

3 yards ahead of second-place finisher Dorothy Hyman. Rudolph ran an astonishing time of 11 seconds flat, but the record was disallowed because of the wind speed.

Even though she hadn't set the official world record, Rudolph had her first gold medal. She stood on the highest level of the victory podium for the first time and listened to the National Anthem.

Her next race was the 200 meters. That race would be tougher on her still tender ankle. Leaning into the curve, she would put much more weight and pressure on the ankle than she did in the 100 meters. Many of the same sprinters she had beaten in the 100 meters would also be racing in the 200. In an early heat, she set an Olympic record of 23.2, the fastest time ever run in the Olympic games. That added to her confidence.

On the day of the final the weather was rainy, but Rudolph started well and came out of the curve far ahead of the field, her taped ankle presenting no problem. She won by 3 yards in a time of 24 flat. She was disappointed by the time but thrilled to have her second gold medal. Only the 4×100-meter relay remained for her.

Unlike the other races, in the relay she

Rudolph won her first gold medal at Rome in the 100 meters.

would not be dependent solely on her own abilities. She and her three Tigerbelle teammates had been working for weeks perfecting the exchanges of the baton between runners that is required in relay races. The first three runners would also have to run fast legs in order to give the USA a chance to beat the favored teams from the Soviet Union, Great Britain and West Germany.

The women from Tennessee State did just that. Martha Hudson ran a strong opening leg and handed off smoothly to Lucinda Williams for the second 100 meters. The American team was leading. Williams kept the lead and passed the baton to Barbara Jones. By the time she approached a waiting Rudolph, Jones had opened up a 2-yard advantage on the second-place West German team. Jutta Heine was running that country's anchor leg. With such a lead, Rudolph would easily hold on for a win.

Just as they had practiced many times before, Rudolph started running as Jones approached with the baton. During the exchange, the baton was bobbled and Rudolph had to pause to firmly grip it. In that split second, the West German team took a two-step lead. Rudolph would have to make up the distance.

By the time Rudolph and Heine came out of the curve, they were even. The two long-legged sprinters matched strides and then Rudolph began to pull away, finishing with her characteristic flair. She had the third gold medal!

In just two weeks, Rudolph quickly became an international star, not simply because she was a winner, but because she won with style. In Italy, fans threw their autograph books onto the track for her to sign. During a post-Olympic tour of Europe, crowds flocked to get a glimpse of her. Stadiums in England, Holland and Germany filled with people anxious to watch the world's fastest woman run. In Cologne, West Germany, police on horseback had to hold back the crowds.

Finally she arrived back in Clarksville for a parade in her honor. Black and white citizens of the town joined together to praise her and celebrate the triumphs of its native daughter. It was the first integrated event ever held in Clarksville.

Rudolph continued to run after the Olympics, and during a meet in Germany in 1961, added the world record that the wind in Rome had denied her. She ran the 100 meters in 11.2 seconds, a record which stood for nearly four years.

Only twenty-one years old, she next had to decide whether to continue to compete and train until the next Olympics in Tokyo, Japan, in 1964. She thought, according to her autobiography, "Look, you already won three gold medals. You go back in 1964, you had better win three more, or even four, or else you're a failure. You lose in 1964, that's what people will remember—the loss, not the three golds in 1960." She decided to retire a winner.

Her influence in the athletic world went beyond the numbers in the record books or the gold medals. Her Olympic coach in 1956, the late Nell Jackson, told Arthur Ashe in his book *A Hard Road to Glory:* "Wilma's accomplishments opened up the real door for women in track because of her grace and beauty. People saw her as beauty in motion."

By her example she demonstrated that a woman could be an athlete and still keep her femininity. She also proved to blacks that they could overcome poverty and discrimination to become the best in the world.

Since Rudolph's retirement, she has remained active in public life. In 1963, when blacks often faced violent opposition to their quest for civil rights, Rudolph strongly supported justice for her race. Showing the same proud profile that crossed the finish line, Rudolph stood among a group of 300 blacks who gathered at a segregated Clarksville restaurant and demanded that they be served.

She has worked as a teacher, a coach, a director of a community center, a fund raiser for the Track and Field Hall of Fame, and the founder and director of her own foundation to help disadvantaged youngsters. In 1977 she wrote her autobiography, *Wilma*, on which an acclaimed television film was based.

Her honors didn't end with the gold medals in 1960. In 1980 she was an inaugural inductee into the Women's Sports Hall of Fame. In 1986 she lit the torch at the Pan American Games, which were held in her present home of Indianapolis, Indiana. And her hometown recently honored her by changing the name of a main road in town to Wilma Rudolph Boulevard.

The little girl who hobbled down the streets of Clarksville had come a long way.

FOR THE EXTRA POINT

Ashe, Arthur. *A Hard Road to Glory: A History of the African-American Athlete Since 1946.* New York: Warner Books, 1988. (Advanced readers.)
Biracree, Tom. *Wilma Rudolph.* New York: Chelsea House Publishers, 1987.
Rudolph, Wilma. *Wilma.* New York: New American Library, 1977. (Advanced readers.)

The 20-year-old from Tennessee left Rome with three gold medals.

WILMA GLODEAN RUDOLPH

WORLD RECORDS

100 METERS

Time	Date	Place
11.3 seconds	September 2, 1960	Rome, Italy
11.2 seconds	July 19, 1961	Stuttgart, West Germany

(The record was tied by Wyomia Tyus of the U.S. on October 15, 1964, and broken on July 9, 1965, by Irena Kirszenstein of Poland, who ran the distance in 11.1 seconds.)

200 METERS

Time	Date	Place
22.9 seconds	July 9, 1960	Corpus Christi, Texas

(The record was tied by Margaret Burvill of Australia on February 22, 1964, and broken on August 8, 1965, by Irena Kirszenstein of Poland, who had a time of 22.8 seconds.)

OLYMPIC MEDAL-WINNING PERFORMANCES

1956 OLYMPICS: MELBOURNE, AUSTRALIA

Medal	Event	Time	Date
Bronze	4 × 100-Meter Relay (with Mae Faggs, Margaret Matthews, and Isabelle Daniels)	44.9 seconds	December 1

1960 OLYMPICS: ROME, ITALY

Medal	Event	Time	Date
Gold	100 Meters	11.0 seconds*	September 2
Gold	200 Meters	24.0 seconds	September 5
Gold	4 × 100-Meter Relay (with Martha Hudson, Lucinda Williams, and Barbara Jones)	44.5 seconds	September 9

*The time was better than the existing world record, but the wind was above the acceptable limit for the record to be counted as official.

Muldowney's dragster often reaches
speeds of 280 miles per hour.

SHIRLEY MULDOWNEY

Queen of the Drag Strip

When a driver is snug in the cockpit of a dragster, protected by a helmet and flame-retardant suit, faced with a clear strip of pavement, it doesn't matter if a man or a woman is behind the wheel. At that point, what's most important is that the driver is a *racer.* And Shirley Muldowney is a racer.

She found early in her life the one thing she really loved—drag racing. In spite of the naysayers who told her over and over that it was a sport for men, not women, she never backed down. She just pushed the gas pedal and beat them to the finish. She focused on her goals as intently as her blue eyes watched the lights on the starting pole before a race. YELLOW, YELLOW, YELLOW, YELLOW, GREEN!

She had beaten the men and earned their respect on her own terms. She had proved that she belonged with them, roaring down a quarter-mile track at 250 miles per hour in a 24-foot-long missile that traveled so fast it needed a parachute to slow it down at the end of a run.

Then in 1984 she had a terrible crash. After a year and a half of surgery and therapy, she started racing again. Three years passed without a national win. People no longer said she couldn't win because she was a woman. They said she couldn't win because she was too old at age forty-nine to drive a dragster. She was washed up, they

said. Since her accident, questions arose about her will to win, something no one had ever doubted before.

Now, in September of 1989, she had advanced to the finals of the Fallnationals at the Firebird International Speedway near Phoenix, Arizona. She focused her eyes again on the lights. YELLOW. Her shiny pink dragster quivered. YELLOW. She'd made it to the finals. YELLOW. But she couldn't be satisfied with second place. YELLOW. She waited for the green light.

Shirley Muldowney was born on June 19, 1940. She grew up in a tough neighborhood in Schenectady, New York, a manufacturing town just a few miles from the state capital, Albany. Her father, Belgium Benedict Roque, was a taxi driver and a professional boxer who fought under the name "Tex Rock." Despite his rough profession, he had an interest in music that he tried to encourage in his daughter. He played the violin and once brought home an accordion for Shirley when she was eight years old.

Her mother, Mae, told *Sports Illustrated* magazine, "It was bigger than she was. Shirley couldn't even carry it."

Shirley's small size made her a target for bullies at school. They teased her, and when they tired of that, they beat her up. Finally, her father told her that she should defend herself. She soon found that when she fought back against those who harassed her, they often backed down. She liked that.

By the time she was thirteen, she lost interest in school and started skipping classes. Her life was more exciting outside the walls of the school. At fifteen, she had a steady boyfriend named Jack Muldowney, a young mechanic who had a reputation as the best hot-rodder in town. Some nights, Shirley would sneak out of the house, and she and Jack would drive to little-used roads outside of town for illegal drag racing, until the police showed up to chase them away.

In 1956, Shirley got her learner's permit and began racing Jack's 1951 Mercury. Her reputation as a hot-rodder grew, and with Jack's mechanical skill coaxing the car to better and better performances, she was beating all the boys from the area. The success she had only made her wish for more. Behind the wheel of a car, she didn't feel small.

Later in 1956, Shirley dropped out of high school and married Jack. Within a year, she and Jack had a son, whom they named John. When Shirley turned nineteen, she and Jack were still racing, but instead of prowling the back streets of upstate New York, they began to enter official professional drag races on weekends at area tracks. Fans and participants at these tracks were often surprised that Shirley was the driver. It was an unusual sight at a drag strip to see the mechanic lean over and kiss the driver before a run, but the Muldowneys were not ashamed of their roles.

They put much of their money into maintaining the car, and it was not always easy to make ends meet. But gradually they began to have some success driving low-budget stock cars, which are basically the same models you see in an auto dealer's showroom.

After six years of racing at small tracks, the Muldowneys decided to move up a class in the sport from a stock car to a **gas dragster**. To race in the Top Gas class required special licensing from the National Hot Rod Association (NHRA), the official governing body of drag racing. The NHRA sets the safety standards and makes rules for the sport. In 1965, Muldowney became the first woman ever licensed by the NHRA to operate a Top Gas dragster. That same year, she also got another important piece of paper: her high school equivalency diploma. She had promised her father she would get her diploma before he died.

Early in her career, Shirley grabbed the attention of racing fans because she was a curiosity: a woman competing in a sport that had been exclusively male. Some fans and other drivers had a hard time accepting that a woman could compete, much less succeed, in drag racing. They often booed her when she appeared on the track. She didn't let such responses discourage her. In fact, the objections even spurred her on to greater successes. She told *Ms.* magazine in 1983, "I really think what kept me going was a mean streak I had. There were all those people who jabbed me—you know, stuck in the knife and broke if off—telling me, 'You can't do this, and you shouldn't do that.' But I discovered that if I had something to get ticked off about, I did a better job."

Gradually, as drag racing people saw that she was a serious and competent racer and not just an oddity, she gained their respect. In another move, Shirley and Jack began racing in the Funny Car division. A Funny Car has the chassis, or frame, and engine of a dragster, topped with a fiberglass body shaped like a regular stock car's. The cars look like stock cars in shape but go much faster.

In 1972, after thirteen years of living in

DRAG TALK

Christmas tree: the vertical stand of lights that signal the drivers when it is time to accelerate from the starting line.

elapsed time: the time it takes for a racer to cover the distance of a quarter-mile (1,320 feet).

gas dragster: a racing car that runs on the same gasoline as standard automobiles.

pit crew: the team of workers a driver hires to repair and service the car before, during, and after a race.

roll cage: the metal frame surrounding the driver that protects the driver from injury in the event of a crash.

motel rooms and touring around the country, Jack grew tired of life on the road. Shirley wanted to race even more, to pursue what she loved to its highest level. The thrill of winning made her even more ambitious. The differences between Jack and her intensified. Jack had got her started in racing, had fueled her love for the sport and had supported her early career, but when she wanted to make it a full-time career, he wasn't ready to go along for the ride. He and Shirley divorced.

In her next career move, Shirley teamed up with a driver named Connie Kalitta, a veteran of the NHRA circuit. Kalitta knew his way around tracks all over the country, and he began serving as Shirley's agent, booking her as "Cha Cha" Muldowney. She was known by that nickname for years, and while it created publicity at the time, she has since decided that it emphasized her gender instead of her driving skills. She has given up the name and despises it today.

By 1973, her son, John, was a teenager and a member of her **pit crew**. She was having success in the Funny Car class. At Indianapolis that year, she had her worst

accident so far. The engine exploded and the subsequent fire caused the goggles she was wearing to melt from her face. Plastic surgery was required to repair the damage to her eyes.

Such an accident might persuade a weaker person to give up, but Muldowney chose not only to keep racing, but to move to even faster cars—Top Fuel dragsters. In this class, the sport of drag racing is at its purest.

These slender speed machines are often called "diggers" or "rails" and are the fastest of all the vehicles approved by the NHRA for racing. They are little more than a huge engine mounted on a thin 24-foot frame, with a seat for the driver, and they commonly reach top speeds over 250 miles per hour. Behind the driver are two enormous tires, called "slicks", which are broad and treadless to get the most traction, or grip on the pavement, especially at the start. On the front of the car, smaller wheels the size of motorcycle tires rest lightly on the ground. While their design is similar, the main difference between a Top Fuel and a Top Gas dragster is in the tank. Top Gas dragsters burn regular gasoline, just like you would buy at the local service station, but Top Fuel cars run on nitromethane, a highly explosive and powerful liquid fuel.

In nearly all drag races, no matter what class, the driver is faced at the start of the race with a vertical column of starting lights called a **"Christmas tree."** Often the driver's reaction to the lights and the traction he or she gets at the start can mean a difference of a couple of hundredths of a second in a quarter-mile run. Drag races are often decided by hundredths of a second.

All through her career, Muldowney has had one of the best starts in the sport. Her reaction time to the Christmas tree consistently gets her away from the start quicker than her opponent. She told *Sports Illustrated:* "I'm not sure if you'd call it a woman's touch or not. I do think women have better reflexes."

Drag racing is a sport of nerves as well as horsepower. Like boxers dancing and shadowboxing on their way to the ring before a bout, drag racers use the burnout pit, which is just a vacant patch of asphalt, to demonstrate to an opponent how powerful their cars are. These crowd-pleasing moves, which envelop the driver in smoke from the tires, also have a practical purpose. One of the racer's crew members pours bleach on the slicks, and when the driver lets out the clutch pedal, the tires spin, squealing and smoking. This heating preparation helps the driver get better traction on the asphalt.

In 1975, Muldowney had broken into the top fifteen drivers on the Winston Top Fuel circuit. She was the runner-up in two national races. The following year, she won the NHRA Springnationals and the Winston World Finals. She managed to attend to her responsibilities as a mother even as she was rising in the sport; John graduated from high school the same week she won her first Top Fuel national.

In 1977, Muldowney finally won the crowning title of drag racing, the Winston championship. The champion is determined by the number of points a driver accumulates for performances in a series of races throughout the year. She captured three national events in a row that year.

She again won the Winston championship in 1980, but in spite of her long, trophy-filled career, she still could not find a major sponsor, a company that offers financial support to drivers in exchange for publicity. Many of the men who had been less successful drivers had sponsors who poured money into their teams in exchange for the publicity of being associated with a driver. They also paint the company's name across the thin frame of their dragsters. She had some minor sponsors, but Muldowney's rail, with its bright pink color and script "Shirley" on the sides, advertised mostly the

driver herself.

Over the years, Muldowney's pink dragster had become her trademark. While she doesn't want to be judged as a "woman' driver, she doesn't deny her femininity. In fact, painting her dragster pink makes it a symbol of pride. She told *Sports Illustrated* "I would be a fool if I didn't paint the car pink. The pink car stands out.... The women like it. Little girls love it.... It's par of an image, that's all the color is. It's feminine. It's a girl's image."

No one was sure why a top driver like Muldowney couldn't get a major sponsor. Some said she was too flashy. Some said it was simply because she was a woman.

In any case, because of the lack of sponsorship, she was forced to enter more races than some of her competitors to make ends meet. This took a greater toll on her car.

Without the financial advantages of sponsorship, she found that she had to do many things herself. Instead of working for a sponsor, she formed her racing team into a business, Shirley Muldowney Enterprises, Inc., and ran it herself, doing the bookkeeping in her hotel room as she traveled around the country.

In 1981, she was a two-time national winner and in 1982, she was winner or runner-up in no fewer than seven national races. This performance made her the Winston Top Fuel champion for the third time, something no one—man or woman—in the history of the sport had ever done. Even "Big Daddy" Don Garlits, who was widely acknowledged as the best driver in the sport, had at that time won only two Winston titles. He and Muldowney had a fierce rivalry over the years. They had roared down the quarter-mile strip side-by-side many times, and at one time Garlits had even kept a tally of his wins over her displayed on the door of his trailer in the pit area.

In 1983, Muldowney's life was the subject of a film entitled *Heart like a Wheel*, which

The color pink became Muldowney's trademark.

depicted her life through 1980. Bonnie Bedelia, the actress who played Muldowney, received an Academy Award nomination for her performance. While the story is an exciting one as told in the movie, Muldowney's biggest challenges and triumphs were still to come.

An incident in 1984 would provide her with the biggest challenge of her life. At the Sanair Speedway outside Montreal, Canada, in June, one of her front tires blew out at about 250 miles per hour, and the inner tube wrapped around her front wheel axle,

flipping the dragster, which rolled 600 feet and ended up in a ditch. Muldowney, strapped into her **roll cage** in the required helmet and fire-retardant suit, nevertheless suffered terrible injuries which required surgery. Her ankle was crushed, her pelvis and legs broken, and she suffered numerous cuts and abrasions. She remained in a hospital in Montreal for 7½ weeks and over the next year required five more operations, in addition to grueling physical therapy and rehabilitation programs. With 17 pins in her legs, she spent most of her time in a wheelchair. Even walking was painful, but she forced herself through it to regain strength in her leg muscles.

She had been in accidents before, but nothing as bad as this. At first she was depressed. She told *Sports Illustrated:* "The whole world had fallen apart in a matter of seconds. Oh, let me tell you, I cried." Her crew chief, Rahn Tobler, who is now her husband, helped to nurse her back to health. From Montreal, she returned to her home in Mt. Clemens, Michigan, to recover.

During this time, she received and answered thousands of get-well notes from her fans. The outpouring of sympathy encouraged her. And even as she sat in a wheelchair recovering, she knew she wanted to sit behind the wheel of a dragster again.

A year and a half after her crash, she stepped onto a drag strip once more to compete in a race at the Firebird track. The crowd was the largest ever at that speedway; over twenty thousand people showed up to welcome Muldowney back.

Because of the accident, she had to make several adjustments to her life and her driving. Her right leg is five-eighths of an inch shorter than her left, so she now walks with a limp. In the dragster, because she could not bend her ankle, the clutch pedal had to be made especially large.

Her answers to the press about the reasons for her return were simple and sincere. "I missed my friends," she said, "I missed my job. I needed the money. It was what I did best."

One positive consequence of the accident was that Goodyear designed a new tubeless tire for the front wheels of dragsters. Such a tire would prevent an accident like the one that happened to Muldowney from occurring again.

She had a new car too, designed by Tobler and her son John, now 28. It sported a rear wing so tall that Muldowney called it the "Kareem wing," after former Los Angeles Laker center Kareem Abdul-Jabbar, who sent Muldowney an autographed

picture when she was recovering. She also acquired a major sponsor, Performance Automotive Wholesale, a company that sells automobile parts by mail.

In her first run since the accident, she clocked a 5.97 for the quarter-mile. Later in the same event she covered the distance at 235.60 miles per hour in 5.59 seconds, which was only three-hundredths of a second slower than her fastest time ever. Even though she won that matchup, she did not advance in the competition. She was back, but her car was not. At the end of the run, the engine blew and she had to withdraw.

A few weeks later in Pomona, California, for the Winternationals, the car was back in shape and so was Muldowney. In a quarterfinal run, she turned in a 5.470, the quickest quarter-mile of her career up to then. She passed through the timing lights at the end of the track at a speed of 252.8 miles per hour. But she lost in the next round to "Big Daddy" Don Garlits when an oil line burst.

She ended up tenth in the year's Winston standings, and in 1987 improved to eighth. That year, although she turned in the fastest speed of her career so far—284.27 miles per hour—she still failed to make the final round of any event, much less win one.

In 1988, in a qualifying round of the Winston World Finals, she had the best **elapsed time** of her career, making the run in 5.151 seconds. She advanced to the quarterfinals of four more races and the semifinals of one, but no further.

At age forty-eight, Muldowney was praised for her courage in attempting a comeback, but many doubted her ability to make it to the top again. Drag racing had changed drastically since veterans like Muldowney and Garlits started racing in the 1950s.

Advances in technology have made the Top Fuelers faster and more powerful. In the last twenty years, drivers have reduced elapsed times by more than a second, from the six-second range to just under five seconds. The speed a Top Fuel dragster reaches has increased by more than 50 miles per hour, from the 230s to the 280s. And the horsepower a digger puts out has risen from 1,500 to 3,500.

The pit area has changed as well. Now after a run, the crew hooks up the dragster to a computer, which examines the performance of the engine and prints out the information for the pit crew to evaluate.

Still, controlling it all is the driver, whose reactions, skill, and courage can make the difference between a win and a loss. Races are still decided by hundredths of a second.

But what of Muldowney's skills? Had they deteriorated since the accident? Had age robbed her of those reflexes that commonly gave her a jump on her opponent at the start? Those questions would be hanging in the air until she won. She was determined

Competing in a "male" sport, Muldowney doesn't give up her femininity.

to answer them with a resounding "No!" But when...?

She had come too far through too much pain to give up. She responded to the doubts with her usual persistence. "I'll drive as long as I can," she said.

In the spring of 1989, Muldowney and her crew sought out the mechanical know-how of another veteran driver, none other than "Big Daddy" Garlits himself. Garlits and Muldowney had gone head-to-head many times in their long careers, and they competed in one of the sport's bitterest rivalries. But after Muldowney's crash in 1984, Garlits viewed his old nemesis more sympathetically, even offering some financial help with her enormous medical expenses. A 1987 crash of his own, which broke a few ribs, forced Garlits into a temporary retirement.

Now after a season of working on Muldowney's car, Garlits and her crew had helped get her to the starting line in the final round of the 1989 Fallnationals at Firebird. But Muldowney was alone behind the wheel, waiting for the timing lights to click down to green.

GREEN! She popped the clutch and spun the wheels, releasing the pent-up horsepower in a swirl of smoke and a blare of noise. Rubber gripped the asphalt and shot the car forward. Through the goggles, all she saw was a gray-blue streak of pavement and sky. She was through the finish line in seconds and the braking parachute trailed behind. It had been a good run. Good enough to win. Shirley Muldowney was in a familiar place, a place where she belonged: the winner's circle.

FOR THE EXTRA POINT

Duden, Jane. *Shirley Muldowney.* Mankato, Minnesota: Crestwood House, 1988.

After a serious crash, Muldowney directed a successful comeback.

SHIRLEY MULDOWNEY

CAREER RECORD IN NATIONAL EVENT FINALS

1989
NorthStar Nationals Runner-up
Heartland Nationals Runner-up
Fallnationals Winner

1983
Winternationals Winner
Springnationals Runner-up
Winston World Finals Winner

1982
Winternationals Runner-up
Gatornationals Winner
Cajun Nationals Runner-up
Springnationals Winner
Grandnational Runner-up
NorthStar Nationals Winner
U.S. Nationals Winner

1981
Gatornationals Winner
Southern Nationals Winner

1980
Winternationals Winner
Springnationals Winner
Fallnationals Winner
Winston World Finals Winner

1979
Cajun Nationals Runner-up

1977
Springnationals Winner
Summernationals Winner
Grandnationals Winner

1976
Springnationals Winner
Winston World Finals Winner

1975
Springnationals Runner-up
U.S. Nationals Runner-up

THREE QUICKEST ELAPSED TIMES
4.962 seconds, 9/29/89, Heartland Nationals, Topeka, Kansas
4.974 seconds, 9/15/89, Keystone Nationals, Reading, Pennsylvania
4.975 seconds, 9/17/89, Keystone Nationals, Reading, Pennsylvania

THREE FASTEST SPEEDS
289.66 miles per hour, 10/6/89, Chief Nationals, Ennis, Texas
288.73 miles per hour, 10/7/89, Chief Nationals, Ennis, Texas
287.72 miles per hour, 8/5/89, Seafair Nationals, Seattle, Washington

Abbott didn't let the lack of a hand prevent him from playing baseball.

JIM ABBOTT

Baseball's Wonder Boy

All parents who are expecting a baby wish for a healthy child. When the baby is born, the first thing many parents do is count the fingers and toes.

On September 19, 1967, when Jim Abbott was born, his parents saw immediately that he was different. He was born without a right hand. The rest of his body was perfect in every way, but his right forearm ended in a nub, from which extended the barest glimmer of a finger.

Some of the terms people use to describe this condition sound negative: a physical *handicap*, a birth *defect*, a *disability*. Jim's parents chose not to treat Jim's situation as a limitation, but as a trait that made him an individual, something that made him special.

They didn't think his lack of a right hand had to limit him from achieving whatever he wanted. He could still be a doctor, or a lawyer, or an athlete.

Mike and Kathy Abbott were both eighteen years old and just out of high school when they had Jim. Even with the responsibility of raising a child, they still managed to complete college. Mike worked as a meatpacker and a car salesman before becoming a sales manager for a beer distributor. Kathy took a job teaching and then went on to law school.

Jim grew up in Flint, Michigan, a town of one hundred sixty thousand. When he was five, his parents had him fitted with an artificial hand with metal hooks. It allowed him to do things like tie his shoes, but he felt even more self-conscious with it than he did without it, so after a while he stopped wearing it.

To make sure that Jim never felt out of place because of his arm, his father encouraged him to be outgoing and friendly. Jim later told the *Los Angeles Times*, "My dad was always pushing me, when I'd see someone new, to walk up to the kid, shake his hand and say, 'Hi, my name is Jim Abbott.' He never wanted me to feel held back because of my hand."

Sports were an important part of life for Jim and his friends. His parents tried to steer him toward soccer, where the absence of one hand wouldn't be such a disadvantage, but Jim loved baseball. They didn't discourage him from trying. His father bought him a glove for his left hand,

and the two of them worked out a system so that they could play catch. To throw the ball, Jim would balance the pocket of the glove on the nubby end of his right forearm while he threw with his left arm. When he completed the throwing motion, he would slip his left hand into the glove to catch the return throw or prepare for fielding.

When his father threw the ball back to him, he would catch it in his gloved left hand, cradle the ball and glove with his right arm, and remove his left hand from the glove, catching the ball as it fell out of the pocket. He was then ready to throw again.

Besides throwing with his father, he would play for hours by himself, hurling a rubber ball against a brick wall near his family's town house. The harder he threw, the quicker the ball bounced back to him, and the faster he was forced to make the switch with the glove.

When enough kids were around in the neighborhood, they played baseball with a tennis ball, using a lawn chair for a strike zone and a miniature bat. Jim played along. No one told him he couldn't play because he had only one hand. So he kept right on playing.

By the time he reached the age for Little League, he had already been making the glove switch for so many years that it became perfectly natural to him. It was the only way he knew how to play. Perhaps because he was forced to do everything with his left arm, it developed great strength. At age eleven, when he pitched in his first Little League game, he fired a **no-hitter**.

As he grew older and the levels he played in became more competitive, opposing teams tried to take advantage of what they perceived as a handicap. When he was a freshman at Flint Central High School, one team **bunted** on him eight straight times, thinking he would have trouble fielding the ball. To Jim it was like scooping up the ball as it came off the brick wall near his home,

and he threw out seven of the eight batters.

He grew steadily through high school, and as a senior he was 6'3" tall and weighed 200 pounds. While he had decided that his primary sport was baseball, he played other sports as well. He was a graceful, fluid athlete. As a junior, he went out for the football team, playing not on the line where catching and throwing aren't important skills, but at quarterback. He was second-string during his junior year, but when the starter was injured during Jim's senior season, he led the team to the semifinals of the state playoffs with a 10–2 record, once

Abbott rests his glove on the nub of his arm before delivering a pitch.

throwing 4 touchdown passes in one game. He also punted for the team and averaged 37.5 yards per kick. In basketball, a sport that would seem to require two hands for ball handling and shooting, Jim led the Central High intramural league in scoring.

But baseball was clearly his best sport, with his strong left arm his greatest asset. The speed of his fastball had increased from about 80 miles per hour as a freshman to 90 miles per hour as a senior. A good major league fastball travels 90 to 95 miles per hour.

By the time he was a senior, the other teams had learned not to bunt on him and frequently couldn't even get the bat on the ball. In the opening game of the season in the spring of 1985, he threw a no-hitter against Swartz Creek High School, striking out 16 batters.

The rest of the season was no less sensational. He threw 3 more no-hitters, including one perfect game where only two balls were hit in fair territory. In $72^{1/3}$ innings pitched, Jim Abbott had 148 strikeouts, an average of better than 2 strikeouts per inning! He allowed only 16 hits all season and finished with a 0.75 **earned run average**.

Catching, throwing, and switching his glove had become so natural that people who came specifically to see him play had trouble picking him out on the field. He looked like any other player.

When he wasn't pitching, Abbott played first base and left field. At the plate, he was a solid hitter. To bat, he balanced his stub on the bat and then wrapped his left hand around both the bat and the stub. Using that technique, Abbott hit for an average of .427. Even more amazing was Abbott's team-leading total of 7 home runs.

Scouts from major league teams had already begun to notice the numbers that the seventeen-year-old from Flint was producing. Every year, the major league teams go through a selection process in which they take turns choosing the best talent from high schools, colleges, and other amateur teams. This is called the amateur "draft." The scouts of a team, after viewing players from all over the country, report back to the management and suggest which players the team should choose. After the draft, the player usually goes into that team's minor league organization for a few years to get experience at a lower level before moving up to the major leagues.

Abbott impressed the Toronto Blue Jays of the American League enough that they drafted him in the 36th, or last, round. They offered him a $50,000 bonus to sign a

---

MOUND TALK

bunt: to bat lightly without swinging so that the ball rolls within the infield. This is usually done as an attempt to advance the runner.

curve ball: a pitch thrown with a spin that will cause the ball to travel in a slightly curving arc on its path to the batter.

earned run average (ERA): a statistic that measures the effectiveness of a pitcher by telling how many runs batters earn from him every nine innings. This statistic is calculated by dividing the number of earned runs by the number of innings pitched and multiplying the total by nine. For example, 111 earned runs ÷ 311 innings pitched = .03569 earned runs per inning. Then .03569 × 9 = 3.21 earned run average. A lower ERA indicates a better pitcher.

no-hitter: a game during which the pitcher allows no opposing batter to reach base on a hit.

off-speed pitch: a ball thrown by the pitcher that is slower than a fast ball, such as a curve ball, and is meant to fool the batter rather than overpower him.

shutout: a game in which the pitcher keeps the opposing team from scoring any runs.

strike zone: the area over home plate in which a pitched ball, if not hit by the batter, is called a strike. By current rules, the strike zone extends from the batter's armpits to his knees.

contract with them, but instead of becoming a professional right away, he decided instead to go to college and play there, remaining an amateur. He reasoned that if he eventually found out he wasn't good enough to play in the major leagues, he would have a college education to fall back on.

He accepted a baseball scholarship to the University of Michigan in Ann Arbor, just 55 miles away from his hometown. Michigan had one of the best college baseball programs in the country and played in one of the toughest conferences, the Big Ten.

Before his freshman year at Michigan, Abbott began to get national attention. CBS Sports highlighted him in a profile that aired on the "NFL Today" show. *People* magazine featured him in an article.

With all the attention on him, he experienced more pressure than the average freshman. For his first two starts, a camera crew from NBC showed up to videotape his performances. He had a hard time putting the ball in the **strike zone**, and coach Bud Middaugh had to take him out of the game.

His next appearance came in relief at a college tournament in Orlando, Florida. When Abbott came into the game in the bottom of the seventh inning, the University of North Carolina had runners on first and third with two out. After Abbott got two strikes on the first batter he faced, the Michigan catcher threw the ball back to Abbott on the mound. As the ball was in the air, the runner on third broke for home. He thought he could steal a run while Abbott was busy switching his glove. But the young pitcher was used to opponents trying such tricks. He caught the ball, made the lightning-fast glove transfer, and threw the runner out, retiring the side. Michigan rallied to win the game, and Abbott got his first collegiate win.

He finished the year with a 6–2 won-lost record, including a win in the Big Ten championship game against the University of Minnesota. Taking over for the

Wolverines' starting pitcher, he worked 6⅔ innings and had 10 strikeouts, his season high. Perhaps the most amazing statistic of his freshman year was this: In 17 fielding chances, he made only one error.

It was a good start to a college career for Abbott, but he found that he still had a lot to learn. In high school he was able to overpower hitters with just his fastball. In college, the hitters were faster and stronger with the bat, so he had to learn to control his fastball more, placing a pitch in a specific location of the strike zone. And he had to learn a curve. He couldn't get college batters out with just one pitch.

His sophomore season demonstrated how far he had progressed as a pitcher. After an opening loss and a game in which he got no decision, Abbott reeled off 9 straight victories, during which he didn't allow an earned run for 35 innings. He finished the season with an 11–3 record and a 2.08 earned run average. The Wolverines finished with a 52–12 record and won their second straight Big Ten title. His teammates named him their most valuable pitcher.

Whatever level Jim Abbott had to reach in order to succeed, he had done it. Along the way, people praised him for being courageous and inspirational. After his splendid sophomore year, the Philadelphia Sports Writers Association gave him its Most Courageous Athlete award in 1987. When Abbott heard himself called courageous, he addressed the topic with typical humility. He told Bill Jauss of *The Chicago Tribune*, "Courage is getting up every day and facing a life-threatening situation. It's much more than fielding bunts. Baseball is just a game."

After the busy spring of a college baseball season, Abbott had a full summer ahead of him. The United States was putting together its national team to compete in the Pan American Games, an Olympic-style competition involving only countries from the Western Hemisphere.

The U.S. team, formed from the best amateur players in the country, would play an international exhibition schedule around the world before the Pan Am Games, which were being held in Indianapolis, Indiana, that year. The competition from the tour and the games would also help decide the team that would play the next summer in the 1988 Olympic Games in Seoul, South Korea.

At the start of the Pan Am tryouts, the coaches of the American team doubted his ability to handle bunts against the experienced international players. One coach ordered players to test Abbott's fielding with a series of bunts. But Abbott had been handling bunts—and doubters—for a long time. He made the team.

The highlight of the team's exhibition tour before the Pan Am Games was a July trip to Havana, Cuba, for seven games against the Cuban national team. Cubans are passionate about baseball, and their team is always strong in international play.

The Cuban fans had heard about Abbott, and when he was scheduled to pitch, over fifty thousand people packed the stands and gave him a standing ovation when he took the mound. He would do more to deserve their applause. The Cuban leadoff hitter was a swift runner named Victor Mesa, and during his first at bat, he hit a high chopper in front of the mound on the third base side. Abbott rushed to his right, caught the ball and threw Mesa out at first. It was a difficult play for any pitcher, and Abbott had made it flawlessly.

When he left the game in the seventh inning with an 8–3 lead, the Cubans gave him another standing ovation. The Americans retained the lead, and Abbott became the first American pitcher in more than two decades to beat the Cuban national team in Cuba.

Among those in attendance at the game was Cuban president Fidel Castro, who was a good enough pitcher in the 1940s to be scouted by the Washington Senators.

During a reception for the American team, Castro extended his left hand for Abbott to shake. During the tour Abbott led the team with an 8–1 record and a 1.70 earned run average.

A month later, Abbott was chosen to carry the American flag during the opening ceremonies of the Pan Am Games. He called his parents in Flint to tell them the good news. On the day of the ceremonies, holding the flag tightly in his left hand, he proudly led the American contingent in the parade of athletes.

In the opening game against Nicaragua, the first batter to face Abbott bunted, and Abbott threw him out with plenty of room to spare. Abbott has often been asked if he thinks bunting against him is a fair way to play. He has said: "The way I look at it, if a batter is weak on an inside pitch, I'll throw inside. If they feel I'm a weak fielder, then they should try to take advantage of me. I think of it as an easy out." The United States beat the Nicaraguans 18–0, as Abbott pitched 5 innings and struck out 6 batters. He also won a more important game against Canada in the semifinals to clinch for the American team both a silver medal in the Pan Am Games and a qualifying spot in the Olympic Games the following summer.

His feats of 1987, both as a collegian and a member of the national team, earned him the Golden Spikes Award as the country's top amateur baseball player. Early in 1988, he found out that he was a finalist for the Sullivan Award, which is given annually to the nation's best amateur athlete. Previous winners included track stars Rafer Johnson and Carl Lewis, swimmer Mark Spitz, and basketball players Bill Bradley and Bill Walton. No baseball player had ever won the honor in its 57 previous years.

As a finalist Abbott was in Indianapolis for the Monday ceremony. He had forgotten that he was supposed to give a speech to his public speaking class at Michigan that day, but he ended up giving a speech anyway that night as he was named winner of the

Abbott pitched the U.S.A.
to victory in the 1988
Seoul Olympics.

award. Turning the praise away from himself, he said, "They probably picked the worst athlete here," and looked at the other finalists, who included such stars as hurdler Greg Foster and basketball player David Robinson. "To be in the company of some of these champions is truly an honor," he said.

Abbott's senior season at Michigan began six days later against the University of Texas, one of college baseball's major powers. Abbott lost that game, but went on to win 8 in a row. During that winning streak he pitched the fifth and sixth **shutouts** of his career and at one point went 24 consecutive innings without allowing an earned run. He finished the season with a 9–3 record and a 3.32 earned run average. Though his numbers were not as good as the year before, he was under more pressure, and opponents concentrated harder, hoping to beat the Sullivan Award winner.

Still, his performance during his senior year earned him awards as the Big Ten Player of the Year for baseball and the conference's Athlete of the Year.

Next up for Abbott was major league baseball's amateur draft. If a player doesn't enter an organization out of high school, he is eligible to be drafted again after three years of college. After all his success, Abbott knew he would be drafted higher than the 36th round this time. And he was right. The California Angels chose him in the first round with the eighth selection. He was one step closer to the goal he had voiced as early as high school—to play in the major leagues.

There were other considerations first, namely the Olympics. His experience with the U.S. national team the summer before made him a logical choice for the Olympic team as well. He was chosen, and the team once again embarked on a worldwide tour to prepare them for the level of competition they would face at the Olympics.

Playing in Japan, Italy, and Cuba, Abbott finished the exhibition tour with an 8–1

record and a 2.55 earned run average, and the team posted a 38–10 record.

Abbott was scheduled to pitch in an early game against Canada, which had one of its strongest teams in many years. He pitched 3 innings and struck out 7 batters as the U. S. won. As many people had predicted, the U. S. ended up in the final game for the gold medal against Japan.

With Abbott on the mound, the U. S. took a 4-1 lead until the bottom of the sixth. At that time Abbott's control began to desert him, and Japan scored twice, once when Abbott walked in a run. In the eighth inning, Japan threatened again. With a runner on first, the Japanese batter hit a sharp one-hopper right back at Abbott. He didn't even have time to make the switch of his glove, which was still balanced on his left arm when the ball hit it and glanced off toward first base, about ten feet away. He jumped off the mound, picked it up, and flipped it to the first baseman in time to get the runner out. Two more ground-outs ended the inning.

Abbott seemed to draw confidence from his play in the eighth. In the ninth, he threw four pitches—three of them resulting in ground balls to the third baseman, who threw out the runner all three times. When the last throw was safely in the glove of the first baseman for the third out of the inning, Abbott leaped into the air, his arms reaching for the sky. His teammates ran to the mound and mobbed him; they all tumbled to the dirt in celebration. When they all stood up, outfielder Mike Fiore held an American flag in the center of the mound, where Abbott had assured them of a gold medal.

Abbott returned home an Olympic hero, but he didn't have much time to enjoy it. He had to begin preparing for spring training in March. The Angels held their training camp in Yuma, Arizona, and that's where Abbott and the other rookies who hoped to make the team would show the manager and coaches what they could do.

The Angels planned to send Abbott to play with their minor league club in Midland, Texas, after spring training. Midland was a double-A team, or two levels below the major leagues. That was a common level for a player to begin his professional career after college.

Once in training camp, however, the Angels soon discovered that Abbott was no common baseball player. In his first spring training game, on a windy day in the Arizona desert, Abbott appeared in the fourth inning against the San Diego Padres and struck out the first batter he faced with an inside fastball. He struck out the next batter, too. After a hitter reached first on an error, Abbott got Tim Flannery, a veteran major leaguer, to ground out to first base. He pitched two more innings, giving up a total of two singles. He allowed no runs and walked no one.

The Angels were also impressed, but they still thought he should start the year at Midland. He needed to work on his **curve ball**, they said.

More impressive than the pitching, however, was the way Abbott handled himself in the face of massive press coverage. He had always dreamed of playing in the majors, and that dream was being charted by hundreds of newspapers, magazines, and television stations from all over the world. Other rookies were able to nurse their ambitions in peace and occasionally escape from the pressure of spring training, but everywhere Abbott went there was another reporter, asking the same questions over and over again. "Do you have trouble with fielding?" "Do you consider yourself courageous?" Still he sat patiently and answered all the questions politely.

Throughout the spring, he continued to shine. He struck out the Oakland A's powerful slugger Jose Canseco. His curves were starting to break more sharply, leaving both right-handed and left-handed hitters flailing with their bats. He

occasionally had trouble throwing in the strike zone, a typical condition with strong left-handers, but his **off-speed pitches** were breaking well. He was developing more quickly than the Angels management had anticipated.

People began to pay attention to his skills rather than his right arm. Reporters began to ask him baseball questions instead of ones about his courage. In addition to making the major leagues, he longed for the day when his lack of a hand would no longer be noticed.

Meanwhile, the Angels were rethinking their plans for Abbott. His fastball was timed at 94 miles per hour in spring training, and he was pitching well against major league competition. He was showing great poise and confidence both on and off the field. They began to think about putting Abbott on their opening-day roster. He had played far better than they had expected, and to send him to the minor leagues might hurt his confidence more than help. Most of all there was the team to think about: If he was one of the best pitchers in the organization, why shouldn't he be in the majors?

Since the institution of the amateur draft in 1965, fewer than twenty pitchers had jumped directly from amateur ball to the big leagues without playing in the minors. Some were famous flops like David Clyde in 1973, who went straight from high school to the Texas Rangers, where he won only 18 games in his career. The most games any of those pitchers won as rookies was 6 by Dick Ruthven of the Philadelphia Phillies in 1973.

Abbott, however, was not a kid just out of high school. In addition to three years with one of the best college programs in the country, he had played two summers of tough international baseball and competed in the Olympics. There was every reason to believe all that experience could be equal to a year in the minors.

The Angels decided to put him in their starting pitching rotation when the season

In 1989 Abbott achieved his lifelong dream of playing in the majors.

opened. He had finally achieved his goal of playing for a major league team.

His spring training debut had been heavily covered by the press, but that was nothing compared to the attention he received for the first regular-season start of his major league career. For the game in Anaheim, California, against the Seattle Mariners, over 150 representatives of the media showed up, including four Japanese television crews. Baseball is a popular sport in Japan, and fans there had followed his career since he defeated their national team in the Olympics. A sellout crowd of 46,847 people including Abbott's father, mother, and brother came to watch.

All the attention created an atmosphere unusual for an early-season game. That night Abbott did not have his best stuff. He lasted 4²/₃ innings, throwing 83 pitches and giving up 6 hits and 6 runs before he was taken out of the game. When he did leave, the crowd gave him a standing ovation.

After the game at a press conference, Abbott remained humble in his assessment of his accomplishments: "I don't think there is anything special about me being in the major leagues. What I've done is not any more triumphant than anybody else's effort. I'm not special."

Like any rookie, Abbott had his ups and downs during his first season. His first win came against the Baltimore Orioles in April, when he pitched 6 innings and gave up 2 runs in a 3–2 victory for the Angels. He threw 2 shutouts during the season, both of them against the Boston Red Sox. In one of those, he outdueled Roger Clemens, one of the best pitchers in baseball, and allowed only 4 hits as the Angels won 4–0. He finished the season with a record of 12–12, thus doubling the win mark for a rookie pitcher who never played in the minor leagues.

He of course accomplished much more than mere numbers could ever measure. Hundreds of letters came in every day, many of them from handicapped kids who were inspired by Abbott not to limit their goals. Many parents of physically challenged younsters wrote to thank him for the example he set.

One of the best examples of his attitude toward his life and accomplishments was related by columnist Scott Ostler in *The Los Angeles Times*. When Abbott was in Seoul for the Olympics, he would carry around his camera to take pictures of all the athletes he admired in the Olympic village. To take a picture, he holds the camera upside down, crooked in his left hand. Abbott said: "People see me do that and they say, 'Hey you gotta turn it around.' They don't realize the pictures come out the same."

Jim Abbott has turned our ideas about handicaps upside down and shown us that people who do things differently can still produce the same result. Whether a pitcher has one hand or two, if he throws three strikes, the batter is out.

FOR THE EXTRA POINT

Ellen E. White. *Jim Abbott: Against All Odds.* New York: Scholastic, 1990.

JAMES ANTHONY ABBOTT

COLLEGE STATISTICS

University of Michigan
Wolverines

Year	Games	IP	H	BB	SO	W	L	SV	ERA
1986	14	50 1/3	49	34	44	6	2	0	4.11
1987	15	86 1/3	71	39	60	11	3	0	2.08
1988	17	97 2/3	88	56	82	9	3	0	3.32
Totals	46	234 1/3	208	129	186	26	8	0	3.03

OLYMPIC STATISTICS
Seoul, South Korea

United States

Year	Games	IP	H	BB	SO	W	L	SV	ERA
1988	2	12	11	5	11	1	0	0	2.25

MAJOR LEAGUE STATISTICS

California Angels

Year	Games	IP	H	BB	SO	W	L	SV	ERA
1989	29	181 1/3	190	74	115	12	12	0	3.92

IP = Innings Pitched
H = Hits
BB = Walks
SO = Strikeouts

W = Wins
L = Losses
SV = Saves
ERA = Earned Run Average

Tom Seaver brought a winning attitude to the laughable Mets.

THE 1969 NEW YORK METS

For much of their early history, the New York Mets were the laughingstock of the sports world. They were the lovable, clumsy buffoons who stumbled around the field, floundered at bat, made mental errors running the bases, and had it all chronicled by the numerous sports writers working for New York newspapers.

In 1962, when the Mets were formed, New Yorkers had been without a National League baseball team for four seasons. In 1957 the owners of the Brooklyn Dodgers and the New York Giants, which were both in the National League, decided to move their teams to the West Coast. There they became the Los Angeles Dodgers and the San Francisco Giants. Fans of those teams in New York were angry; the teams they had cheered for years were uprooted and transplanted 3,000 miles away. The only baseball team left in town was the American League's New York Yankees.

The Yankees were perhaps the most powerful dynasty in all of sports. Year after year they had great players, Hall of Famers, who led them to the American League pennant. They were hated by many Giant and Dodger fans. When those two teams left the city, the Yankees thought they would pick up some of their baseball-hungry fans. In fact, the Yankees' attendance dropped the year after the Giants and Dodgers left.

Clearly there was room for another team in New York. A wealthy group of New Yorkers decided to fill that void and formed the Metropolitan Baseball Club of New York. From this corporate name came the team name, the "Mets."

To manage the Mets, the owners hired

seventy-two-year-old Casey Stengel, a legendary baseball figure. He had managed the Yankees to ten American League pennants but was better known for his way with words. He loved to talk to sportswriters and rarely found himself without a quip on his lips. He was, however, serious about baseball. He would help the team get on its feet, and his personality would capture fan interest in New York.

Stengel had been active in baseball since 1912, when he played with the Brooklyn Dodgers. He was fired as the Yankee manager in 1960, and when the Mets called, he was happy to return to baseball. He was certainly the central figure in making the Mets lovable during their terrible early years. With his rubbery face twisted into all kinds of contortions, he humorously commented on his team's bad luck. The sportswriters could always count on Casey for a good quote about the game.

The early Mets were a ragged bunch of no-names and journeymen players with a few aging stars thrown in. When the team was admitted into the National League, the Mets were allowed to choose players from the other teams' rosters, players those teams didn't want. The Mets' first pick was a catcher named Hobie Landrith. When the press corps asked Stengel why he chose Landrith, he said, "If you don't have a catcher, you have a lot of passed balls."

One player more than any other would come to be identified with the Mets' early futility. His name was Marvin Eugene Throneberry, a big first baseman who had been playing in the Yankee organization. His initials even spelled out M.E.T. He quickly became a crowd favorite, more for his bumbling in the field than his heroics at the plate.

"Marvelous Marv," as Throneberry came to be known, was a balding thirty-year-old Tennessean who had the ability to laugh at himself. When another Met made an error, Throneberry would say, "What are you trying to do, steal my fans?" Once when

Throneberry hit a triple, the opposing team claimed that he hadn't touched first base, and he was called out. Stengel came out of the dugout to argue the call, and the umpire said, "I hate to tell you this, Casey, but he missed second base, too." Replied Casey, "Well, I know he touched third because he's standing on it."

Their first season started off badly when the Mets lost a game in St. Louis, returned to New York and, on Friday the Thirteenth no less, lost their first home game to Pittsburgh. They lost seven more in a row. In the last game of that season, Joe Pignatano, later a coach with the 1969 Mets, hit into a rare triple play, where three outs are made on one batted ball. That season the Mets won 40 games and lost 120, more losses than any other major league team in baseball this century. They finished in last place out of ten teams, 60½ games behind the first-place Giants. (The number of "games" by which a team trails the leader in the baseball standings is computed by adding the difference in the losses between the two teams to the difference in the wins between the two and dividing the total by two. The Giants won 103 games and lost 62 games [(103-40) + (120-62)] / 2 = 60.5 games behind.) Any way you add it up, the Mets stunk.

Among Stengel's comments about his team would be the frequently used adjective "amazin'," so the team became known in the headlines and to the fans as the "Amazin' Mets." That name would lose its sarcastic tone in 1969 and be replaced by a more appropriate adjective: "Miracle Mets."

The next few seasons were little better than the first. In 1963, they finished in last place again, 48 games out of first. One of their pitchers, Roger Craig, lost 18 straight games. In 1964, they finished with a record of 53–109 and ended in last place again. Stengel was still the manager, but he was nearing age seventy-five, and the team of lovable losers was beginning to wear thin on the fans. They wanted a winner, not a comedy act.

Midway through the 1965 season, Stengel broke his hip and had to retire from baseball. Under a temporary manager, the Mets finished the year once again in last place, 47 games behind the Dodgers.

There was some reason for Met fans to hope for better things to come. The organization had been bringing good young talent up through the minor leagues. In 1966, for the first time, the Mets finished out of the National League cellar, in ninth place, 7½ games ahead of the Chicago Cubs.

One minor leaguer in particular impressed the Mets. George Thomas Seaver, a twenty-one-year-old right-handed fastball pitcher, had struck out 188 batters in 210 innings for the Mets' Jacksonville, Florida, team. He was promoted to the Mets in 1967 and had a winning record (16–13) with a team that was as unlucky as ever, falling back into last place and losing 101 games. Seaver was named the National League Rookie of the Year.

Almost as important as his pitching was his attitude. He was a serious young man who didn't like to lose. Though people still made jokes about the Mets, Seaver didn't laugh. Just as serious and determined was catcher Jerry Grote, a tough Texan obtained in a trade with Houston before the 1966 season.

Most important, in 1968 the Mets had a new manager, Gil Hodges, who had played first base for the Brooklyn Dodgers and for the Mets' dismal 1962 team. Hodges was a quiet and patient man, but also a stern disciplinarian who would not put up with disagreements on his team. The average age of the Met team in 1968 was twenty-six years old, and Hodges felt the young players needed a strong hand, not a friend. He saw his role as that of a teacher.

Though the Mets were on their way to another losing season and a ninth-place finish in 1968, they posted their best record ever, 73–89.

The team was especially strong "up the middle," that is, at catcher, pitcher, second base, shortstop, and center field. Grote was already the best defensive catcher in the league, and by changing his swing at the plate, he improved his **batting average** from .195 in 1967 to .282 the following year.

Seaver was the star of the pitching staff, but in 1968 he was joined by Jerry Koosman, a strong left-handed Minnesota farm boy who surprised everyone with a 19–12 record, including seven shutouts, tying a league rookie record. Veteran Don Cardwell had joined the Mets in 1966, and he provided them with a steady starter to relieve the young arms. Young fireballing Nolan Ryan, the only Met from the 1969 team still playing today, was only 6–9 in 1968, but he struck out 133 batters in 134 innings. The pitching staff's 2.72 earned run average was fourth-best in the league.

Bud Harrelson played shortstop for the Mets, and his 1968 batting average of .219 was offset by his spectacular fielding. Grote told Maury Allen in the book *After the*

DIAMOND TALK

batting average: a statistic that measures a player's skill in hitting. It is calculated by dividing the number of hits by the number of times at bat. For example, 185 hits ÷ 456 at bats = .406 batting average. A higher average indicates a better hitter.

line drive: a sharply hit ball that travels in almost a straight line only a few feet off the ground.

platoon: to split playing time at one position on the field between two or more players.

sacrifice bunt: a ball hit deliberately into the infield that forces the fielder to throw the bunter out at first base, allowing another runner already on base to advance.

warning track: the dirt area around the outfield that alerts fielders backing up for a fly ball that they are nearing the wall.

Miracle: "We had something no other club had and that was Buddy Harrelson. I would tell our pitchers that all they had to do was get the batter to hit the ball to Harrelson. He was the most sure-handed shortstop I ever saw."

At second base the Mets started Ken Boswell, who through the first half of the season in 1968 was hitting well enough to be talked about as a Rookie of the Year candidate. He finished the year with a batting average of .261.

The Mets' center fielder, Tommie Agee, had been an American League Rookie of the Year in 1966 with the Chicago White Sox. After two bad seasons, he was traded to the Mets. He struggled for much of 1968, hitting only .217, but he was an excellent fielder, and Hodges thought he needed a year to adjust to the new team and league.

Late in the 1968 season, after a game in Atlanta, Hodges complained of chest pains and was taken to the hospital. The doctors discovered that he had suffered a mild heart attack. He spent four weeks in the hospital but vowed to return to manage his team the next year.

In February, 1969, when the Mets' spring training camp opened in St. Petersburg, Florida, there was Hodges on the sidelines, looking as serious as ever. How the news of the attack affected his team in 1968, we don't know. How the sight of him in their spring training dugout encouraged them, we can only guess. But we do know that the team that returned to the field in 1969 was different, more mature than the one that finished 1968.

Sportswriters and other observers predicted a 1969 season little better than the seven that had preceded it. The oddsmakers had the Mets as a 100-to-1 shot to win the World Series.

In 1969 the National League expanded, adding two more teams—the Montreal Expos and the San Diego Padres. Twelve teams competing for one pennant would be unwieldy, so the league decided to divide the teams into two divisions of six teams each. The Mets would compete in the East Division with Chicago, St. Louis, Philadelphia, Montreal, and Pittsburgh. Cynics joked that the Mets therefore were spared a ninth- or tenth-place finish by the structure; the worst they could do would be sixth. And that's where many predicted the Mets would finish.

The opening game did little to disprove that belief. The Mets lost for the eighth straight year on Opening Day, this time to the newly formed Expos. The early part of the season was just as uninspiring. Near the end of May the Mets had a record of 18–23, had lost five straight, and were in fifth place, nine games behind the division-leading Chicago Cubs.

After winning a close, extra-inning game against San Diego, the Mets faced the Giants and Dodgers for three games each at home in Shea Stadium. Because of fan ties to those teams, the Mets always got a big crowd when they would come to visit. This time, though, the fans were cheering for the Mets.

Seaver delighted the fans by pitching the Mets to a 4–3 victory over the Giants. The win seemed to spark the team. They took the two remaining games from the Giants by close scores. The Dodgers were next.

Koosman pitched the opener against the Dodgers and held them to one run as the Mets won 2–1. As quickly as they had dropped five in a row, the Mets won five in a row and improved to 23–23 for a .500 winning percentage. A winning percentage is calculated by dividing the number of wins by the total number of games played. Hodges told them before the season started that they couldn't be considered a serious contender for the title until they reached the .500 mark. It was the first time the Mets were that good with that much of the season behind them.

The winning didn't stop there. And the Mets kept finding unlikely heroes. For the next game against the Dodgers, the team brought in Jack DiLauro, a twenty-one-year-old pitcher who had been playing with their minor league team in Tidewater, Virginia. He kept the streak going by shutting out the Dodgers for nine innings, and the Mets went on to win the game 1–0 in 15 innings.

The team traveled west and swept three games from San Diego and won one more in San Francisco for a team-record eleven victories in a row. They had improved their record from 18–23 to 29–23 and moved securely into second place in the division behind the Cubs.

The battle with the Cubs was to continue all season. In May, when the Mets had visited the Cubs in Chicago, batters from both teams had been hit by pitches, resulting in a brawl. The rivalry continued

when the Cubs came to Shea Stadium in July. The Mets were behind in the series opener 3–1 as they came to bat in the bottom of the ninth inning, their last chance to tie or win the game.

Boswell reached second base on a fielding error by the center fielder. Up next was Donn Clendenon, a thirty-three-year-old slugger picked up by the Mets in a trade with the Montreal Expos in June. He gave the Mets the one element they lacked in their batting order—a veteran power hitter.

With Boswell on second, Clendenon smashed a pitch to the left-center-field wall, which the center fielder caught but dropped as he slammed into the fence. When the ball came back into the infield, Boswell was on third and Clendenon on second. The Mets'

Agee's great fielding in the Series justified Hodges' faith in him.

Cleon Jones, who was leading the league with a .360 average, doubled in both runners to tie the score. A few moments later, first baseman Ed Kranepool slashed a single to left and drove Jones home with the winning run. It was a rousing victory for the Mets. Amazin'.

Those Met fans who weren't believers earlier began to come out to the stadium. The next night, Shea Stadium was packed with fifty-eight thousand fans, the most ever to see a Met home game. Seaver proceeded to mow down batter after batter. For eight innings, every Cub Seaver faced returned to the dugout. The pitcher's control was perfect. Going into the ninth inning, the Mets had a 4–0 lead and Seaver was throwing a perfect game, which happens when no batter reaches base. This is so rare an occurrence that only sixteen have been thrown since 1901.

The crowd noise was deafening as Seaver took the mound in the ninth. The first batter tried to bunt for a base hit, but Seaver skipped off the mound and threw him out. Next up was Jimmy Qualls, a rookie who had hit the ball hard in two other at bats. Seaver let fly with a high fastball, and Qualls lashed it to left field for a single. Seaver's shoulders slumped as the ball dropped in. The crowd quieted and then gave Seaver a standing ovation.

The addition of Donn Clendenon gave the team a veteran slugger.

He had come within two outs of perfection. Still, he went right back to the mound and finished off the game, getting the last two outs. He said in *After the Miracle*, "It was pivotal for us because it showed the Cubs how good we were."

The Mets visited Chicago the next week, where they won two of three from the home team. More unlikely heroes emerged. Infielder Al Weis, who had hit only four home runs in 611 games before 1969, hit two home runs in two days against the Cubs to cement the Met victories.

In spite of their inspiring wins over the Cubs, the Mets followed that series with a month-long slump, during which they lost more games than they won. The Cubs, shrugging off the losses to the Mets, continued to win and by August 15 had opened up a 9½-game lead. The Mets were in third place.

Returning home after a road trip, the Mets won nine of ten games to pull within five games of the Cubs. There were, however, only thirty-nine games remaining in the season. Time was running out.

When the Cubs came into Shea for a must-win two-game series, the Mets had made up 2½ games and were only 2½ behind. The Mets pitching stars, Seaver and Koosman, were scheduled. In the first game Koosman struck out 13 Cubs and the Mets won 3–2. The next night, the Mets' hitters gave Seaver a big lead and he coasted to a 7–1 win. The Cubs' lead had shrunk to ½ game. A combination of a Met win and a Cub loss would put the Mets into first place for the first time in their history.

Montreal, the team that had spoiled the Mets' Opening Day, came in for a doubleheader. The first game went into extra innings, and in the twelfth, Jones scored the winning run on a Boswell single to give the Mets a 3–2 win. In the second game, as Nolan Ryan pitched a four-hitter to beat the Expos, the crowd—and the Mets—kept their eyes on the scoreboard for the result of the Chicago-Philadelphia game.

Shortly after 10 p.m., the news flashed in Shea Stadium: The Cubs had lost! The Mets had taken over first!

Two days later the Mets swept another doubleheader, this time against Pittsburgh, when the starting pitchers, Koosman and Cardwell, drove in the only runs in identical 1–0 victories. In 1962 the Amazin' Mets found strange ways to lose. In 1969 the Mets were amazin' in a different way; they found unusual ways to win.

Perhaps the oddest win of the season came in a game on September 15 against St. Louis. That night the Cardinals' star pitcher, Steve Carlton, struck out 19 Mets to set a major league record. The Mets, however, won the game when Ron Swoboda hit a two-run home run twice in the game to account for all of the Mets' scoring in a 4–3 win.

The Mets kept winning, and on September 24 they clinched the Eastern Division title with a 6–0 win over St. Louis. Though security had been increased for the game, the fans at Shea stormed onto the field in celebration. They uprooted the bases. They cut up the sod to take home souvenirs. There was mayhem on the field and champagne in the clubhouse. The Mets, the butt of countless jokes even up to the year before, were champions.

Few thought they would be champions of anything other than the National League East. Their pitching had been superb all year, but their hitting was erratic. Jones finished the year with a .340 average, but no one else on the team hit over .300. The Mets' opponents in the National League Championship Series, the Atlanta Braves, were loaded with sluggers like Hank Aaron and Orlando Cepeda.

All year the Mets had never depended on just one player. They had proved themselves with their teamwork. Hodges didn't like to **platoon**—that is, alternate players at certain positions—but this season he did, to the advantage of the team. The combinations worked beautifully. At third base he paired

Fans joined the celebration when the Mets won the 1969 Eastern Division title.

the oldest player on the team (Ed Charles) with the youngest (Wayne Garrett), and the Mets benefited from the exuberance of Garrett and the steady experience of Charles. At first base he platooned Clendenon, the most recent addition to the Mets, and Ed Kranepool, who had been with the team since the dark days of 1963.

By the time the National League Championship Series with Atlanta opened, the Mets were as tight as a team could be. This closeness and confidence made the play-off, which was a best-of-five-games series, a runaway. While the Mets' pitching faltered, the hitting exploded. Seaver was not sharp in the first game, but the Mets scored five runs in the top of the eighth to pull out a 9–5 win. In the second game, the Mets scored in each of the first five innings and went on to an 11–6 victory. At Shea for the third game, light-hitting infielders Garrett and Boswell hit homers and the Mets wrapped up the series 7–4.

Their opponents in the World Series, however, were more formidable: the Baltimore Orioles. They had won 109 games and boasted some of the finest players in the game in Frank and Brooks Robinson, Boog Powell (37 home runs), and future Met manager Davey Johnson. On the mound, the Orioles were at least the equal of the Mets with Jim Palmer, Mike Cuellar and Dave McNally. Their staff had a 2.83 earned run average, the best in baseball. Would the Mets' miracle end?

The Orioles' first at bat, seemed to answer that question with a definitive "Yes!" Leadoff hitter Don Buford knocked Seaver's second throw over the right-field fence for a home run. The Orioles cruised to a 4–1 win.

In the second game, Koosman brought the high-flying Birds to earth. For six innings, he didn't allow the powerful Orioles a hit. Clendenon had given him a one-run lead in the top of the fourth. In the seventh inning, the Orioles tied the game with a single, a stolen base and another single.

As the Mets had done all year, their lesser names performed heroics when necessary. With two out in the ninth, Charles, Grote, and Weis all singled to put the Mets up by one run. The lead held, and the Mets evened the Series at one game apiece.

The Series moved to New York. In the first World Series game ever played at Shea Stadium, Agee, the leadoff batter for the Mets, knocked a Palmer pitch out of the park. Met pitcher Gary Gentry helped his cause when he batted in two runs in the second with a double. The Mets had a 3–0 lead in the game.

Agee would prove just as resourceful in the field. In the fourth inning with two on base, Oriole catcher Elrod Hendricks hit a long fly to left center field which Agee sprinted over to get. He timed his run perfectly, caught the ball and crashed dramatically into the fence. But he held on to the ball; it remained in the webbing of his glove.

Gentry began having control problems in the seventh and walked three straight batters. With two outs, Ryan came in, and

FOR THE EXTRA POINT

Aaseng, Nathan. *Baseball's Brilliant Managers*. Minneapolis: Lerner, 1982.
Aaseng, Nathan. *Baseball's Finest Pitchers*. Minneapolis: Lerner, 1980.
Allen, Maury. *After the Miracle*. New York: Franklin Watts, 1989. (Advanced readers.)
Creamer, Robert W. *Stengel: His Life and Times*. New York: Simon and Schuster, 1984. (Advanced readers.)
Honig, Donald. *The New York Mets: The First Quarter Century*. New York: Crown Publishers, Inc., 1986. (Advanced readers.)
Lang, Jack and Peter Simon. *The New York Mets: Twenty-five Years of Baseball Magic*. New York: Henry Holt and Company, 1986. (Advanced readers.)
Rothaus, James R. *The New York Mets*. Mankato, Minnesota: Creative Education, 1987.

Oriole center fielder Paul Blair connected on a pitch and sent it to deep left center field. Agee again ran after it. Just before the ball came down on the dirt on the **warning track,** he went into a one-knee slide and caught the ball inches off the ground. His two catches prevented at least five runs from scoring, and the Mets won 5–0.

Seaver was ready for another try in the fourth game, and he pitched brilliantly. But so did his counterpart, Cuellar. Clendenon provided the only Met run with a homer in the second inning, so Seaver took a 1–0 lead into the ninth. Frank Robinson and Boog Powell singled to put runners at first and third. Then came the play remembered more than any other in this World Series. Brooks Robinson hit a slicing **line drive** that Swoboda raced after. He dove for the ball headfirst, and it landed in his glove for the out. Robinson tagged up on the play and scored, but Swoboda squelched an Oriole rally.

Met magic reached its season peak in the bottom of the next inning. With a man on first, little-used catcher J. C. Martin tried a **sacrifice bunt,** a strategy in which the batter puts the ball in play long enough to make an out so that the runner moves up one base. The pitcher fielded the ball and threw toward first, but the ball hit Martin on the wrist and bounced away into right field. The runner scored on the play, and the Mets had a victory. They led the Series 3–1.

To many of America's baseball fans, the Mets' World Series lead was as remarkable as the moon landing, which had happened in July. One more game and the Mets would be World Champions.

The Orioles jumped out to a 3–0 lead on Koosman in the fifth game. McNally was shutting down the Met machine, but the New Yorkers had one more miracle in their pockets. In the sixth inning, Jones was at bat when a pitch came low in the dirt at his feet. The ball bounced away into the Met dugout. Jones claimed the ball hit him on the foot and argued that he should be awarded first base. The umpire disagreed. Hodges emerged from the dugout and showed the umpire a ball with a black smudge on it. Hodges said the smudge was shoe polish. The umpire was convinced and Jones went to first. The next batter, Clendenon, promptly hit a homer to bring the Mets within one run. Weis, the unlikely slugging hero from the Cub series, later hit a home run to tie the game. In the bottom of the eighth, the Mets scored twice more to take a 5–3 lead.

In the top of the ninth, the crowd began to clap and cheer wildly as the Mets moved closer to the improbable championship. The clapping subsided when Frank Robinson walked. Powell grounded to second, and the Mets got one out but couldn't turn the double play. Brooks Robinson then flied out. The crowd resumed their clapping and cheering. One out to go. The batter was Davey Johnson, who later became manager of the 1986 World Champion Mets. He lifted a long fly ball to center field, which Cleon Jones camped under. The ball landed firmly in his glove, and he dropped to one knee. The Mets had won the World Series!

The team that had never finished higher than next-to-last was the world champion. They turned the laughter into cheers. What was at the heart of the miracle? As Casey Stengel himself said, "You can see they believe in each other. The Mets are amazin'."

1969 NEW YORK METS

WORLD SERIES STATISTICS

Batting

Player/Position	Games	AB	R	H	2B	3B	HR	RBI	BA
J. Grote, C	5	19	1	4	2	0	0	1	.211
C. Jones, OF	5	19	2	3	1	0	0	0	.158
T. Agee, OF	5	18	1	3	0	0	1	1	.167
B. Harrelson, SS	5	17	1	3	0	0	0	0	.176
R. Swoboda, OF	4	15	1	6	1	0	0	1	.400
E. Charles, 3B	4	15	1	2	1	0	0	0	.133
D. Clendenon, 1B	4	14	4	5	1	0	3	4	.357
A. Weis, 2B	5	11	1	5	0	0	1	3	.455
J. Koosman, P	2	7	0	1	1	0	0	0	.143
A. Shamsky, OF	3	6	0	0	0	0	0	0	.000
E. Kranepool, 1B	1	4	1	1	0	0	1	1	.250
T. Seaver, P	2	4	0	0	0	0	0	0	.000
K. Boswell, 2B	1	3	1	1	0	0	0	0	.333
G. Gentry, P	1	3	0	1	1	0	0	2	.333
R. Gaspar, OF	3	2	1	0	0	0	0	0	.000
W. Garrett, 3B	2	1	0	0	0	0	0	0	.000
D. Dyer, PH	1	1	0	0	0	0	0	0	.000
J. C. Martin, PH	1	0	0	0	0	0	0	0	.000
Totals	5	159	15	35	8	0	6	13	.220

AB = At Bats   2B = Doubles   RBI = Runs Batted In
R = Runs   3B = Triples   BA = Batting Average
H = Hits   HR = Home Runs

Pitching

Pitcher	Games	IP	H	BB	SO	W	L	SV	ERA
J. Koosman	2	17²/₃	7	4	9	2	0	0	2.04
T. Seaver	2	15	12	3	9	1	1	0	3.00
G. Gentry	1	6²/₃	3	5	4	1	0	0	0.00
R. Taylor	2	2¹/₃	0	1	3	0	0	1	0.00
N. Ryan	1	2¹/₃	1	2	3	0	0	1	0.00
D. Cardwell	1	1	0	0	0	0	0	0	0.00
Totals	5	45	23	15	28	4	1	2	1.80

IP = Innings Pitched   BB = Walks   W = Wins   SV = Saves
H = Hits   SO = Strikeouts   L = Losses   ERA = Earned Run Average

INDEX